THE VAMPIRE'S ASSISTANT

THE SAGA OF DARREN SHAN
BOOK 2

THE SAGA OF DARREN SHAN

THE DEMONATA

Also Available on Audio

DARREN SHAN

THE VAMPIRE'S ASSISTANT

THE SAGA OF DARREN SHAN
BOOK 2

HarperCollins *Children's Books*

Madam Octa's on the Web... and so is Darren Shan!
For all things freaky, check out the official
Darren Shan website at www.darrenshan.com

First published in Great Britain by HarperCollins *Children's Books* in 2000
HarperCollins *Children's Books* is a division of HarperCollins*Publishers* Ltd
77-85 Fulham Palace Road, Hammersmith
London W6 8JB

The HarperCollins *Children's Books* website address is:
www.harpercollinschildrensbooks.co.uk

19

Text copyright © Darren Shan 2000

ISBN-13   978 0 00 675513 5
ISBN-10   0 00 675513 5

The author asserts the moral right to
be identified as the author of the work.

Printed and bound in Great England by
Clays Ltd, St Ives plc

For:

Granny and Grandad – tough old fogeys

OBEs (Order of the Bloody Entrails) to:
Caroline 'tracker' Paul
Paul 'the pillager' Litherland

Heads off to:
Biddy 'Jekyll' and Liam 'Hyde'
Gillie 'grave robber' Russell
The hideously creepy HarperCollins gang
and
Emma and Chris (from 'Ghouls Are Us')

INTRODUCTION

MY NAME'S Darren Shan. I'm a half-vampire.

I wasn't born that way. I used to be ordinary. I lived at home with my parents and younger sister, Annie. I enjoyed school and had lots of friends.

I liked reading horror stories and watching scary movies. When a freak show came to town, my best mate, Steve Leopard, got tickets and we went. It was great, really spooky and weird. A super night out.

But the weirdest part came after the show. Steve recognized one of the characters from the show ... he'd seen a drawing of him in an old book and knew he was— a *vampire*. He stuck around after the show and asked the vampire to turn *him* into one, too! Mr Crepsley – the vampire – would have, but he found out Steve's blood was evil, and that was the end of that.

Or it *would* have been the end, except *I* stuck around, too, to see what Steve was up to.

I wanted nothing to do with vampires, but I'd always loved spiders – I used to keep them as pets – and Mr Crepsley had a poisonous performing spider, Madam Octa, which could do all sorts of great tricks. I stole her and left a note for the vampire, saying I'd tell people about him if he came after me.

To cut a long story short, Madam Octa bit Steve and he ended up in hospital. He would have died, so I went to Mr Crepsley and asked him to save Steve. He agreed, but in return *I had to become a half-vampire and travel with him as his assistant!*

I ran away after he'd turned me into a half-vampire (by pumping part of his own horrible blood into me) and saved Steve, but then I realized I was hungry for blood, and was afraid I'd do something terrible (like bite my sister) if I stayed at home.

So Mr Crepsley helped me fake my death. I was buried alive and then, in the dead of night, with no one around, he dug me up and we set off together. My days as a human were over. My nights as a vampire's assistant had begun.

CHAPTER ONE

IT WAS a dry, warm night, and Stanley Collins had decided to walk home after the Scouts' meeting. It wasn't a long walk — less than two kilometres — and though the night was dark, he knew every step of the way as surely as he knew how to tie a reef knot.

Stanley was a Scout Master. He loved the Scouts. He'd been one when he was a boy, and kept in contact when he grew up. He'd turned his three sons into first-rate Scouts and, now that they'd grown up and left home, he was helping the local kids.

Stanley walked quickly to keep warm. He was only wearing shorts and a T-shirt, and even though it was a nice night, his arms and legs were soon covered in goosebumps. He didn't mind. His wife would have a lovely cup of hot chocolate and currant buns waiting for him when he got home. He'd enjoy them all the more after a good, brisk walk.

Trees grew along both sides of the road home, making it very dark and dangerous for anyone who wasn't used to it. But Stanley had no fears. On the contrary, he loved the night. He enjoyed listening to the sound of his feet crunching through the long grass and briars.

Crunch. Crunch. Crunch.

He smiled. When his sons were young, he'd pretend there were monsters lying in wait up in the trees as they walked home. He'd make scary noises and shake the leaves of low-hanging branches when the boys weren't looking. Sometimes they'd burst into screams and run for home at top speed, and Stanley would follow after them, laughing.

Crunch. Crunch. Crunch.

If he was having trouble getting to sleep at night, he would imagine the sounds of his feet as they made their way home, and that always helped him drift off into a happy dream.

It was the nicest sound in the world, as far as Stanley was concerned, better than all the music of Mozart and Beethoven.

Crunch. Crunch. Crunch.

Snap.

Stanley stopped and frowned. That had sounded like a stick breaking, but how could it have been? He would have felt it if he'd stepped on a twig. And there were no cows or sheep in the nearby fields.

He stood still for about half a minute, listening curiously. When there were no more sounds, he shook his head and smiled. It had been his imagination playing tricks. He'd tell the wife about it when he got home and they'd have a good laugh.

He started walking again.

Crunch. Crunch. Crunch.

There. Back to the familiar sounds. There was nobody else about. He would have heard more than a single branch snapping if there was. Nobody could creep up on Stanley J. Collins. He was a trained Scout Master. His ears were as sharp as a fox's.

Crunch. Crunch. Crunch. Crunch. Cru—

Snap.

He stopped again, the fingers of fear tightening around his beating heart.

That hadn't been his imagination. He'd heard it, clear as a bell. A twig snapping, somewhere overhead. And before it snapped: had there been the slightest rustling sound, as if something was moving?

Stanley gazed up at the trees but it was too dark to see. There could have been a monster the size of a car up there and he wouldn't have been able to spot it. Ten monsters. A hundred! A thou—

Oh, that was silly. There were no monsters in the trees. Monsters didn't exist. Monsters weren't real. It was a squirrel or an owl, something ordinary like that.

Stanley raised a foot and began to bring it down.

Snap.

His foot hung in the air and his heart pounded quickly. That was no squirrel! The sound was too sharp. Something *big* was up there. Something that *shouldn't* be up there. Something that had never been there before. Something that—

Snap!

The sound was closer this time, lower down, and all of a sudden Stanley could stand it no longer. He ran.

Stanley was a large man, but fairly fit for his age. Still, it had been a long time since he'd run this fast, and after a hundred metres he was out of breath and had a stitch in his side.

He slowed to a halt and bent over, gasping for air.

Crunch.

His head shot up.

Crunch. Crunch. Crunch.

There were footsteps coming towards him! Slow, heavy footsteps. He listened, terrified, as they came closer and closer. Had the monster leapt ahead of him through the trees? Had it climbed down? Was it coming to finish him off? Was ...

Crunch. Crunch.

The footsteps stopped and Stanley was able to make out a figure. It was smaller than he'd expected, no bigger than a boy. He straightened up, gathered his courage about him like a cloak, and stepped forward for a better look.

It *was* a boy! A small, frightened-looking boy, dressed in a dirty suit.

Stanley smiled and shook his head. What a fool he'd been! The wife would have a field day when he told her about this.

"Are you OK, lad?" Stanley asked.

The boy didn't answer.

Stanley didn't recognize the youngster, but a lot of new families had moved into the area recently. He no longer knew every child in the neighbourhood.

"Can I help you?" he asked. "Are you lost?"

The boy shook his head slowly. There was something strange about him, something that made Stanley feel uneasy. It might have been the effect of the darkness and shadows, but the boy looked very pale, very thin, very ... *hungry*.

"Are you all right?" Stanley asked, stepping closer. "Can I—"

SNAP!

The sound came from directly overhead, loud and menacing.

The boy leapt back quickly, out of the way.

Stanley just had time to glance up and spot a huge red shape which might have been a bat, slashing its way down through the branches of the trees.

And then the red monster was on him. Stanley opened his mouth to scream, but before he could, the monster's hands — *claws?* — clamped over his mouth. There was a brief struggle, then Stanley was sliding to the floor, unconscious, unseeing, unknowing.

Above him, the two creatures of the night moved in for the feed.

CHAPTER TWO

"IMAGINE A man his age wearing a Scout's uniform," Mr Crepsley snorted as he turned our victim over.

"Were you ever in the Scouts?" I asked.

"They did not have them in my day," he replied.

He patted the man's meaty legs and grunted. "Plenty of blood in this one," he said.

I watched as Mr Crepsley searched the leg for a vein, then cut it open – a small slice – using one of his fingernails. As soon as blood oozed out, he clamped his mouth around the cut and sucked. He didn't believe in wasting any of the "precious red mercury", as he sometimes called it.

I stood uncertainly by his side as he drank. This was the third time I'd taken part in an attack, but I still wasn't used to the sight of the vampire sucking blood from a helpless human being.

It had been almost two months since my "death", but I was having a tough time adjusting to the change. It was hard to believe my old way of life was finished, that I was a half-vampire and could never go back. I knew I had to eventually leave my human side behind. But it was easier said than done.

Mr Crepsley lifted his head and licked his lips.

"A good vintage," he joked, shuffling back from the body. "Your turn," he said.

I took a step forward, then stopped and shook my head.

"I *can't*," I said.

"Do not be stupid," he growled. "You have shied away twice already. It is time you drank."

"I can't!" I cried.

"You have drunk animal blood," he said.

"That's different. This is a human."

"So what?" Mr Crepsley snapped. "*We* are not. You have to start treating humans the same as animals, Darren. Vampires cannot live on animal blood alone. If you do not start drinking human blood, you will grow weak. If you continue to avoid it, you will die."

"I know," I said miserably. "You've explained it to me. And I know we don't hurt those we drink from, not unless we drink too much. But ..." I shrugged unhappily.

He sighed. "Very well. It is hard, especially when you are only a half-vampire and the hunger is not so great. I will let you abstain this time. But you must feed soon. For your own sake."

He returned to the cut and cleaned away the blood — which had been leaking out while we were talking — from around the man's leg. Then he worked up a mouthful of spit and slowly let it dribble over the cut. He rubbed it in with a finger, then sat back and watched.

The wound closed and healed. Within a minute there was nothing left apart from a small scar that the man probably wouldn't notice when he awoke.

That's how vampires protect themselves. Unlike in the movies, they don't kill people when they drink, not unless they are starving, or get carried away and go too far. They drink in small doses, a bit here, a bit there. Sometimes they attack people out in

14

the open, as we had just done. Other times, they creep into bedrooms late at night, or into hospital wards, or police cells.

The people they drink from hardly ever know they've been fed on by a vampire. When this man woke, he would remember only a falling red shape. He wouldn't be able to explain why he'd passed out or what had happened to him while he was unconscious. If he found the scar, he'd be more likely to think it was the mark of aliens than a vampire.

Hah. *Aliens!* Not many people know that vampires started the UFO stories. It was the perfect cover. People all over the world were waking up to find strange scars on their body, and were blaming it on imaginary aliens.

Mr Crepsley had knocked the Scout Master out with his breath. Vampires can breathe out a special kind of gas, which makes people faint. When Mr Crepsley wanted to send someone to sleep, he breathed into a cupped fist, then held his hand over the person's nose and mouth. Seconds later, they were out for the count, and wouldn't wake for at least twenty or thirty minutes.

Mr Crepsley examined the scar and made sure it had healed correctly. He took good care of his victims. He seemed to be a nice man, from what I'd seen of him — apart from the fact that he was a vampire!

"Come," he said, standing. "The night is young. We will go find a rabbit or a fox for you."

"You don't mind me not drinking from him?" I asked.

Mr Crepsley shook his head. "You will drink eventually," he said. "When you are hungry enough."

"*No*," I said silently behind him, as he turned to walk away. "I won't. Not from a human. I'll never drink from a human. *Never!*"

CHAPTER THREE

I AWOKE early in the afternoon, as usual. I'd gone to bed shortly before dawn, the same time as Mr Crepsley. But while he had to stay asleep until night fell again, I was free to rise and move about in the daylight world. It was one of the advantages of being only a half-vampire.

I fixed a late breakfast of marmalade on toast — even vampires have to eat normal food; blood alone won't keep us going — and settled down in front of the hotel television. Mr Crepsley didn't like hotels. He usually slept out in the open, in an old barn or a ruined building or a large crypt, but I was having none of that. I told him straight-up after a week of sleeping rough that I'd had enough of it. He grumbled a bit, but gave way in the end.

The last two months had passed very quickly, because I'd been so busy learning about being a vampire's assistant. Mr Crepsley wasn't a good teacher, and didn't like repeating himself, so I had to pay attention and learn fast.

I was very strong now. I could lift enormous weights and crush marbles to pieces with my fingers. If I shook hands with a human I had to take care not to break the bones in their fingers. I could do chin-ups all night long, and could throw a metal ball further than any grown-up. (I measured my throw one day, then checked in a book and discovered I'd set a new world record! I was excited at first, but then realized I couldn't tell anybody about it. Still, it was nice to know I was a world champion.)

My fingernails were really thick, and the only way I could shorten them was with my teeth: clippers and scissors were no good on my new, tough nails. They were a nuisance: I kept ripping my clothes when I was putting them on or taking them off, and digging holes in my pockets when I stuck my hands in.

We'd covered a lot of distance since that night in the cemetery. First we'd fled at top vampire speed, me on Mr Crepsley's back, invisible to human eyes, gliding across the land like a couple of high-speed ghosts. That's called *flitting*. But flitting is tiring work, so after a couple of nights we began taking trains and buses.

I don't know where Mr Crepsley got the money for our travel and hotels and food. He had no wallet that I could see and no bank cards, but every time he had to pay for something, out came the cash.

I hadn't grown fangs. I'd been expecting them to sprout, and had been checking my teeth in the mirror every night for three weeks before Mr Crepsley caught me.

"What are you doing?" he asked.

"Looking for fangs," I told him.

He stared at me for a few seconds, then burst out laughing. "We do not grow fangs, you ass!" he roared.

"But ... how do we bite people?" I asked, confused.

"We do not," he told me, still laughing. "We cut them with our nails and suck the blood out. We only use our teeth in emergencies."

"So I won't grow fangs?"

"No. Your teeth will be harder than any human's, and you will

17

be able to bite through skin and bone if you wish, but it is messy. Only stupid vampires use their teeth. And stupid vampires tend not to last very long. They get hunted down and killed."

I was a bit disappointed to hear that. It was one of the things I liked most about those old vampire movies: the vampires had looked so cool when they'd bared their fangs.

But, after some thought, I decided I was better off without the fangs. The fingernails making holes in my clothes were bad enough. I would have been in real trouble if my teeth had grown and I'd started cutting chunks out of my cheeks as well!

Most of the old vampire stories were untrue. We couldn't change shape or fly. Crosses and holy water didn't hurt us. All garlic did was give us bad breath. Our reflections could be seen in mirrors, and we cast shadows.

Some of the myths were true though. A vampire couldn't be photographed or filmed with a video camera. There's something odd about vampire atoms, which means all that comes out on film is a dark blur. I could still be photographed, but you wouldn't get a clear photo of me, no matter how good the light.

Vampires were friendly with rats and bats. We couldn't turn into them, as some books and films claimed, but they liked us – they knew from the smell of our blood that we were different to humans – and often cuddled up to us while we were sleeping or came around looking for scraps of food.

Dogs and cats, for some reason, hated us.

Sunlight *would* kill a vampire, but not quickly. A vampire could walk about during the day, if he wrapped up in lots of clothes. He'd tan quickly, and start to go red within a quarter of an hour. Four or five hours of sunlight would kill him.

A stake through the heart would kill us, of course, but so would a bullet or a knife or electricity. We could drown or be crushed to death or catch certain diseases. We were tougher to

18

kill than normal people, but we weren't indestructible.

There was more I had to learn. Loads more. Mr Crepsley said it would be years before I knew everything and was able to get along by myself. He said a half-vampire who didn't know what he was doing would be dead within a couple of months, so I had to stick to him like glue, even if I didn't want to.

When the toast and marmalade were finished, I sat and bit my nails for a few hours. There wasn't anything good on TV, but I didn't want to go outside, not without Mr Crepsley. We were in a small town, and people made me nervous. I kept expecting them to see through me, to know what I was and to come after me with stakes.

When night fell, Mr Crepsley emerged and rubbed his belly. "I am starving," he said. "I know it is early, but let us head out now. I should have taken more of that silly Scout-man's blood. I think I will track down another human." He looked at me with one raised eyebrow. "Maybe you will join me this time."

"Maybe," I said, though I knew I wouldn't. It was the one thing I'd sworn I would never do. I might have to drink the blood of animals to stay alive, but I would never feast on one of my own kind, no matter what Mr Crepsley said, or how much my belly rumbled. I was a half-vampire, yes, but I was also half-human, and the thought of attacking a living person filled me with horror and disgust.

CHAPTER FOUR

Blood ...

Mr Crepsley spent much of his time teaching me about blood. It's vital to vampires. Without it we grow weak and old and die. Blood keeps us young. Vampires age at a tenth the human rate (for every ten years that pass vampires only age one), but without human blood, we age even quicker than humans, maybe twenty or thirty years in the space of a year or two. As a half-vampire, who aged at a fifth the human rate, I didn't have to drink as much human blood as Mr Crepsley — but I would have to drink some to live.

The blood of animals — dogs, cows, sheep — keeps vampires ticking over, but there are some animals they — *we* — can't drink from: cats, for instance. If a vampire drinks a cat's blood, he might as well pour poison down his throat. We also can't drink from monkeys, frogs, most fish and snakes.

Mr Crepsley hadn't told me the names of all the dangerous animals. There were loads, and it would take time to learn which were safe and which weren't. His advice was to always ask before I tried something new.

Vampires had to feed on humans once a month or so. Most

feasted once a week. That way, they didn't have to take much blood. If you only fed once a month, you had to drink a lot of blood in one go.

Mr Crepsley said it was dangerous to go too long without drinking. He said the thirst could make you drink more than you meant to, and you were likely to end up killing the person you drank from.

"A vampire who sups frequently can control himself," he said. "One who drinks only when he must will end up sucking wildly. The hunger inside us must be fed to be controlled."

Fresh blood was best. If you drank from a living human, the blood was full of goodness and you didn't need to take very much. But blood began to go sour when a person died. If you drank from a dead body, you had to drink a lot more.

"The general rule is, never drink from a person who has been dead more than a day," Mr Crepsley explained.

"How will I know how long a person's been dead?" I asked.

"The taste of the blood," he said. "You will learn to tell good blood from bad. Bad blood is like sour milk, only worse."

"Is drinking bad blood dangerous?" I asked.

"Yes. It will sicken you, maybe turn you mad or even kill you."

Brrrr!

We could bottle fresh blood and keep it for as long as we liked, for use in emergencies. Mr Crepsley had several bottles of blood stored in his cloak. He sometimes had one with a meal, as if it was a small bottle of wine.

"Could you survive on bottled blood alone?" I asked one night.

"For a while," he said. "But not in the long run."

"How do you bottle it?" I asked curiously, examining one of the glass bottles. It was like a test-tube, only the glass was slightly darker and thicker.

"It is tricky," he said. "I will show you how it is done, the next time I am filling up."

Blood ...

It was what I needed most, but also what I feared most. If I drank a human's blood, there was no going back. I'd be a vampire for life. If I avoided it, I might become a human again. Perhaps the vampire blood in my veins would wear out. Maybe I wouldn't die. Maybe only the vampire in me would die, and then I could return home to my family and friends.

It wasn't much of a hope – Mr Crepsley had said it was impossible to become human again, and I believed him – but it was the only dream I had to cling to.

CHAPTER FIVE

DAYS AND nights passed, and we moved on. We wandered from towns to villages to cities. I wasn't getting on very well with Mr Crepsley. Nice as he was, I couldn't forget that he was the one who'd pumped vampire blood into my veins and made it impossible for me to stay with my family.

I hated him. Sometimes, during the day, I'd think about driving a stake through his heart while he was sleeping, and hitting off on my own. I might have, too, except I knew I couldn't survive without him. For the moment I needed Larten Crepsley. But when the day came that I could look after myself ...

I was in charge of Madam Octa. I had to find food for her and exercise her and clean out her cage. I didn't want to – I hated the spider almost as much as I hated the vampire – but Mr Crepsley said I was the one who'd stolen her, so I could look after her.

I practised a few tricks with her every now and then, but my heart wasn't in it. She didn't interest me any more and as the weeks passed I played with her less and less.

The one good thing about being on the road was being able to visit loads of places I hadn't been before, seeing all sorts of sights. I loved travelling. But, since we travelled at night, I didn't get to see much of our surroundings!

One day, while Mr Crepsley was sleeping, I got tired of being indoors. I left a note on the TV, in case I wasn't back when he woke, then set off. I had very little money, and no idea where I would go, but that didn't matter. Just getting out of the hotel and spending some time by myself was wonderful.

It was a large town but fairly quiet. I checked out a few toy stores and played some free computer games in them. I'd never been very good on computers before, but with my new reflexes and skills, I was able to do pretty much anything I wanted.

I raced through levels of speed games, knocked out every opponent in martial arts tournaments, and zapped all the aliens from the skies in sci-fi adventures.

After that I toured the town. There were plenty of fountains and statues and parks and museums, all of which I examined with interest. But going around the museums reminded me of Mum – she loved taking me to museums – and that upset me: I always felt lonely and miserable when I thought of Mum, Dad or Annie.

I spotted a group of boys my age playing hockey on a tarmac quad. There were eight players on each side. Most had plastic sticks, though a few had wooden ones. They were using an old white tennis ball as a puck.

I stopped to watch and, after a few minutes, one of the boys came to size me up.

"Where are you from?" he asked.

"Out of town," I said. "I'm staying at a hotel with my father." I hated calling Mr Crepsley that but it was the safest thing to say.

"He's from out of town," the boy called back to his mates, who had stopped playing.

"Is he part of the Addams Family?" one of them shouted back, and they all laughed.

"What's that supposed to mean?" I asked, offended.

"Have you looked at yourself in a mirror lately?" the boy said.

I glanced down at my dusty suit and knew why they were laughing: I looked like something out of *Oliver Twist*.

"I lost the bag with my normal clothes," I lied. "These are all I have. I'm getting new stuff soon."

"You'd want to," the boy smiled, then asked if I could play hockey. When I said I could, he invited me to play with them.

"You can be on my team," he said, handing me a spare stick. "We're six-two down. My name's Michael."

"Darren," I said in reply, testing the stick.

I rolled up the legs of my trousers and checked my laces were tied properly. While I was doing that, the opposition scored another goal. Michael cursed loudly and dragged the ball back to the centre.

"You want to help touch-off?" he asked me.

"Sure."

"Come on, then," he said, tapped the ball to me and moved ahead, waiting for me to pass back.

It had been a long time since I'd played hockey – at school, in PE, we'd usually have to choose between hockey and football, and I never passed up a chance for a game of footie – but with the stick in my hands and the ball at my feet, it seemed like only yesterday.

I knocked the ball from left to right a few times, making sure I hadn't forgotten how to control it, then looked up and focused on the goal.

There were seven players between me and the goalkeeper. None of them rushed to tackle me. I guess they felt there was no need, being five goals up.

I set off. A big kid – the other team's captain – tried blocking me, but I slipped around him easily. I was past another two before they could react, then dribbled round a fourth. The fifth player slid in with his stick at knee level, but I jumped over him with ease, dummied the sixth and shot before the seventh and final defender could get in the way.

Even though I hit the ball quite softly, it went much harder than the goalie was expecting and flew into the top right-hand corner of the goal. It bounced off the wall and I caught it in the air.

I turned, smiling, and looked back at my team-mates. They were still in their own half, staring at me in shock. I carried the ball back to the halfway line and set it down without saying a word. Then I turned to Michael and said, "Seven-three."

He blinked slowly, then smiled. "Oh yes!" he chortled softly, then winked at his team-mates. "I think we're going to enjoy this!"

I had a great time for a while, controlling the course of play, rushing back to defend, picking players out with pin-point passes. I scored a couple of goals and set up four more. We were leading nine-seven, and coasting. The other team hated it, and had made us give them two of our best players, but it made no difference. I could have given them everybody except our goalkeeper and still knocked the stuffing out of them.

Then things got nasty. The captain of the other team – Danny – had been trying to foul me for ages, but I was too quick for him and danced around his raised stick and stuck-out legs. But then he began to punch my ribs and stand on my toes and slam his elbows into my arms. None of it hurt me, but it annoyed me. I hate sore losers.

The crunch came when Danny pinched me in a *very* painful place! Even vampires have their limits. I gave a roar and crouched down, wincing from the pain.

Danny laughed and sped away with the ball.

I rose after a few seconds, mad as hell. Danny was halfway down the pitch. I set off after him. I brushed the players between us aside — it didn't matter if they were on his team or mine — then slid in behind him and swiped at his legs with my stick. It would have been a dangerous tackle if it had come from a human. Coming from a half-vampire ...

There was a sharp snapping sound. Danny screamed and went down. Play stopped immediately. Everybody in the quad knew the difference between a yell of pain and a scream of real agony.

I got to my feet, already sorry for what I'd done, wishing I could take it back. I looked at my stick, hoping to find it broken in two, hoping that had been what made the snapping noise. But it wasn't.

I'd broken both of Danny's shin-bones.

His lower legs were bent awkwardly and the skin around the shins was torn. I could see the white of bone in amongst the red.

Michael bent to examine Danny's legs. When he rose, there was a horrified look in his eyes.

"You've cracked his legs wide open!" he gasped.

"I didn't mean to," I cried. "He squeezed my ..." I pointed to the spot beneath my waist.

"You broke his legs!" Michael shouted, then backed away from me. Those around him backed away as well.

They were *afraid* of me.

Sighing, I dropped my stick and left, knowing I'd make matters worse if I stayed and waited for grown-ups to arrive. None of the boys tried to stop me. They were too scared. They were terrified of me ... Darren Shan ... a *monster*.

CHAPTER SIX

IT WAS dark when I got back. Mr Crepsley was up. I told him we should skip town straight away, but didn't tell him why. He took one look at my face, nodded and started gathering our belongings.

We said little that night. I was thinking how rotten it was to be a half-vampire. Mr Crepsley sensed there was something wrong with me, but didn't bother me with questions. It wasn't the first time I'd been sulky. He was getting used to my mood-swings.

We found an abandoned church to sleep in. Mr Crepsley lay out on a long pew, while I made a bed for myself on a pile of moss and weeds on the floor.

I woke early and spent the day exploring the church and the small cemetery outside. The headstones were old and many were cracked or covered with weeds. I spent several hours cleaning a patch of them, pulling weeds away and washing the stones with water I fetched from a nearby stream. It kept my mind off the hockey game.

A family of rabbits lived in a nearby burrow. As the day went by, they crept closer, to see what I was up to. They were curious little fellows, especially the young ones. At one point, I pretended to be asleep and a couple edged closer and closer, until they were only half a metre away.

When they were as close as they were likely to get, I leapt up and shouted "Boo!" and they went running away like wildfire. One fell head over heels and rolled away down the mouth of its burrow.

That cheered me up greatly.

I found a shop in the afternoon and bought some meat and veg. I set a fire when I returned to the church, then fetched the pots and pans bag from beneath Mr Crepsley's pew. I searched among the contents until I found what I was looking for. It was a small tin-shaped pot. I carefully laid it upside-down on the floor, then pressed the metal bulge on the top.

The tin mushroomed out in size, as folded-in panels opened up. Within five seconds it had become a full-sized pot, which I filled with water and stuck on the fire.

All the pots and pans in the bag were like this. Mr Crepsley got them from a woman called Evanna, long ago. They weighed the same as ordinary cookware, but because they could fold up small, they were easier to carry around.

I made a stew, as Mr Crepsley had taught me. He believed everybody should know how to cook.

I took leftover bits of the carrots and cabbage outside and dropped them by the rabbit burrow.

Mr Crepsley was surprised to find dinner – well, it was breakfast from his point of view – waiting for him when he awoke. He sniffed the fumes from the bubbling pot and licked his lips.

"I could get used to this," he smiled, then yawned, stretched and ran a hand through the short crop of orange hair on his head. Then he scratched the long scar running down the left side of his face. It was a familiar routine of his.

I'd often wanted to ask how he got his scar, but I never had. One night, when I was feeling brave, I would.

There were no tables, so we ate off our laps. I got two of the folded-up plates out of the bag, popped them open and fetched the knives and forks. I served up the food and we tucked in.

Towards the end, Mr Crepsley wiped around his mouth with a silk napkin and coughed awkwardly.

"It is very nice," he complimented me.

"Thank you," I replied.

"I ... um ... that is ..." He sighed. "I never was very good at being subtle," he said, "so I will come right out and say it: what went wrong yesterday? Why were you so upset?"

I stared at my almost empty plate, not sure if I wanted to answer or not. Then, all of a sudden, I blurted out the whole story. I hardly took a breath between the start and finish.

Mr Crepsley listened carefully. When I was done, he thought about it for a minute or two before speaking.

"It is something you must get used to," he said. "It is a fact of life that we are stronger than humans, faster and tougher. If you play with them, they will be hurt."

"I didn't mean to hurt him," I said. "It was an accident."

Mr Crepsley shrugged. "Listen, Darren, there is no way you can stop this happening again, not if you mix with humans. No matter how hard you try to be normal, you are not. There will always be accidents waiting to happen."

"What you're saying is, I can't have friends any more, right?" I nodded sadly. "I'd figured that out by myself. That's why I was so sad. I'd been getting used to the idea of never being able to go back home to see my old friends, but it was only yesterday that I realized I'd never be able to make new ones either. I'm stuck with *you*. I can't have any other friends, can I?"

He rubbed his scar and pursed his lips. "That is not true," he said. "You can have friends. You just have to be careful. You——"

"That's not good enough!" I cried. "You said it yourself; there will always be an accident waiting to happen. Even shaking hands is dangerous. I could cut their wrists open with my nails!"

I shook my head slowly. "No," I said firmly. "I won't put people's lives in danger. I'm too dangerous to have friends any more. Besides, it's not like I can make a true friend."

"Why not?" he asked.

"True friends don't keep secrets from one another. I could never tell a human that I was a vampire. I'd always have to lie and pretend to be someone I'm not. I'd always be afraid he'd find out what I was and hate me."

"It is a problem every vampire shares," Mr Crepsley said.

"But every vampire isn't a child!" I shouted. "What age were you when you were changed? Were you a man?" He nodded. "Friends aren't that important to adults. My dad told me that grown-ups get used to not having loads of friends. They've work and hobbies and other stuff to keep them busy. But my friends were the most important thing in my life, apart from my family. Well, you took my family away when you pumped your stinking blood into me. Now you've ruined the chances of my ever having a proper friend again.

"Thanks a lot," I said angrily. "Thanks for making a monster out of me and wrecking my life."

I was close to tears, but didn't want to cry, not in front of him. So I stabbed at the last piece of meat on my plate with my fork and rammed it into my mouth, where I chewed upon it fiercely.

Mr Crepsley was quiet after my outburst. I couldn't tell if he was angry or sorry. For a while, I thought I'd said too much. What if he turned around and said, "If that is the way you feel, I will leave you"? What would I do then?

31

I was thinking of apologizing when he spoke in a soft voice and surprised me.

"I am sorry," he said. "I should not have blooded you. It was a poor call. You were too young. It has been so long since I was a boy, I had forgotten what it was like. I never thought of your friends and how much you would miss them. It was wrong of me to blood you. Terribly wrong. I ..."

He trailed off into silence. He looked so miserable, I almost felt sorry for him. Then I remembered what he'd done to me and I hated him again. Then I saw wet drops at the corners of his eyes, which might have been tears, and felt sorry for him once more.

I was very confused.

"Well, there's no use moaning about it," I finally said. "We can't go back. What's done is done, right?"

"Yes," he sighed. "If I could, I would take back my terrible gift. But that is not possible. Vampirism is for ever. Once somebody has been changed, there is no changing back.

"Still," he said, mulling it over, "it is not as bad as you think. Perhaps ..." His eyes narrowed thoughtfully.

"Perhaps what?" I asked.

"We *can* find friends for you," he said. "You do not have to be stuck with me all the time."

"I don't understand." I frowned. "Didn't we just agree it wasn't safe for me to be around humans?"

"I am not talking about humans," he said, starting to smile. "I am talking about people with special powers. People like us. People you can tell your secrets to ..."

He leant across and took my hands in his.

"Darren," he said, "what do you think about going back and becoming a member of the Cirque Du Freak?"

CHAPTER SEVEN

THE MORE we discussed the idea, the more I liked it. Mr Crepsley said the Cirque performers would know what I was and would accept me as one of their own. The line-up of the show often changed, and there was nearly always someone who would be around my own age. I'd be able to hang out with them.

"What if I don't like it there?" I asked.

"Then we leave," he said. "I enjoyed travelling with the Cirque, but I am not crazy about it. If you like it, we stay. If you do not, we hit the road again."

"They won't mind me tagging along?" I asked.

"You will have to pull your weight," he replied. "Mr Tall insists on everybody doing something. You will have to help set up chairs and lights, sell souvenirs, clean up afterwards, or do the cooking. You will be kept busy, but they will not over-work you. We will have plenty of time for our lessons."

We decided to give it a go. At least it would mean a proper bed every night. My back was stiff from sleeping on floors.

Mr Crepsley had to find out where the show was before we could set off. I asked him how he was going to do that. He told me he was able to home in on Mr Tall's thoughts.

"You mean he's telepathic?" I asked, remembering what Steve had called people who could talk to each other using only their brains.

"Sort of," Mr Crepsley said. "We cannot speak to each other with our thoughts but I can pick up his ... *aura*, you could call it. Once I locate that, tracking him down will be no problem."

"Could I locate his aura?" I wanted to know.

"No," Mr Crepsley said. "Most vampires – along with a few gifted humans – can, but half-vampires cannot."

He sat down in the middle of the church and closed his eyes. He was quiet for about a minute. Then his eyelids opened and he stood.

"Got him," he said.

"So soon?" I asked. "I thought it would take longer."

"I have searched for his aura many times," Mr Crepsley explained. "I know what to look for. Finding him is as easy as finding a needle in a haystack."

"That's supposed to be hard, isn't it?"

"Not for a vampire," he grunted.

While we were packing to leave, I found myself gazing around the church. Something had been bothering me, but I wasn't sure whether I should mention it to Mr Crepsley or not.

"Go on," he said, startling me. "Ask whatever it is that is on your mind."

"How did you know I wanted to ask something?" I gawped.

He laughed. "It does not take a vampire to know when a child is curious. You have been bursting with a question for ages. What is it?"

I took a deep breath. "Do you believe in God?" I asked.

Mr Crepsley looked at me oddly, then nodded slowly. "I believe in the gods of the vampires."

I frowned. "Are there vampire gods?"

"Of course," he said. "Every race has gods: Egyptian gods, Indian gods, Chinese gods. Vampires are no different."

"What about heaven?" I asked.

"We believe in Paradise. It lies beyond the stars. When we die, if we have lived good lives, our spirits float free of the earth, to traverse the stars and galaxies, and come at last to a wonderful world at the other side of the universe – Paradise."

"And if they don't live good lives?"

"They stay here," he said. "They remain bound to earth as ghosts, doomed to wander the face of this planet for ever."

I thought about that. "What's a *good life* for a vampire?" I asked. "How do they make it to Paradise?"

"Live cleanly," he said. "Do not kill unless necessary. Do not hurt people. Do not spoil the world."

"Drinking blood isn't evil?" I asked.

"Not unless you kill the person you drink from," Mr Crepsley said. "And even then, sometimes, it can be a good thing."

"Killing someone can be *good*?" I gasped.

Mr Crepsley nodded seriously. "People have souls, Darren. When they die, those souls go to heaven or Paradise. But it is possible to keep a part of them here. When we drink small amounts of blood, we do not take any of a person's essence. But if we drink lots, we keep part of them alive within us."

"How?" I asked, frowning.

"By draining a person's blood, we absorb some of that person's memories and feelings," he said. "They become part of us and we can see the world the way they saw it, and remember things which might otherwise have been forgotten."

"Like what?"

He thought a moment. "One of my dearest friends is called Paris Skyle," he said. "He is very old. Many centuries ago, he was friends with William Shakespeare."

"*The* William Shakespeare – the guy who wrote the plays?"

Mr Crepsley nodded. "Plays and poems. But not all of Shakespeare's poetry was recorded; some of his most famous verses were lost. When Shakespeare was dying, Paris drank from him – Shakespeare asked him to – and was able to tap into those lost poems and have them written down. The world would have been a poorer place without them."

"But ..." I stopped. "Do you only do that with people who ask, and who are dying?"

"Yes," he said. "It would be evil to kill a healthy person. But to drink from friends who are close to death, and keep their memories and experiences alive ..." He smiled. "That is very good indeed.

"Come," he said then. "Brood about it on the way. We must be off."

I hopped on Mr Crepsley's back when we were ready to leave, and off we flitted. He still hadn't explained how he could move so fast. It wasn't that he ran quickly; it was more like the world slipped by as he ran. He said all full vampires could flit.

It was nice, watching the countryside drift away behind us. We ran up hills and across vast plains, faster than the wind. There was complete silence while we were flitting and nobody ever noticed us. It was as if we were surrounded by a magic bubble.

While we flitted I thought about what Mr Crepsley had said, about keeping people's memories alive by drinking from them. I wasn't sure how that would work, and made up my mind to ask him more about it at a later date.

Flitting was hard work; the vampire was sweating and I could see him starting to struggle. To help, I took out a bottle of human blood, uncorked it and held it to his lips so he could drink.

He nodded his silent thanks, wiped the sweat from his brow, and continued.

Finally, as the sky was beginning to lighten, he slowed to a halt. I hopped down off his back and looked around. We were in the middle of a country road, fields and trees all around us, not a house to be seen.

"Where's the Cirque Du Freak?" I asked.

"A few kilometres further ahead," he said, pointing. He was kneeling down, panting for breath.

"Did you run out of steam?" I asked, unable to keep the giggles out of my voice.

"No," he glared. "I could have made it, but did not want to arrive looking flushed."

"You'd better not rest too long," I warned him. "Morning's on its way."

"I know precisely what time it is!" he snapped. "I know more about mornings and dawns than any living human. We have plenty of time on our side. A whole forty-three minutes yet."

"If you say so."

"I *do*." He stood, annoyed, and began to walk. I waited until he was a bit in front, then ran ahead of him.

"Hurry up, old man," I jeered. "You're getting left behind."

"Keep it up," he growled. "See what it gets you. A clip around the ear and a boot up the pants."

He started trotting after a couple of minutes, and the two of us jogged along, side by side. I was in good spirits, happier than I'd been for months. It was nice having something to look forward to.

We passed a ragged bunch of campers on our way. They were starting to wake up and move around. A couple waved to us. They were funny looking people: long hair, strange clothes, weighed down with fancy earrings and bracelets.

There were banners and flags all over the camp. I tried reading them, but it was hard to focus while I was jogging, and I didn't want to stop. From what I could gather, the campers had something to do with a protest against a new bypass.

The road was very curvy. After the fifth bend, we finally spotted the Cirque Du Freak, nestled in a clearing by the banks of a river. It was quiet – everyone was sleeping, I imagined – and, if we'd been in a car and not looking for the vans and tents, it would have been easy to miss.

It was an odd place for the circus to be. There was no hall or big tent for the freaks to perform in. I figured this must be a resting point between two towns.

Mr Crepsley weaved between the vans and cars with confidence. He knew exactly where he was going. I followed, less sure of myself, remembering the night I crept past the freaks and stole Madam Octa.

Mr Crepsley stopped at a long silver van and knocked on the door. It opened almost immediately and the towering figure of Mr Tall was revealed. His eyes looked darker than ever in the dim light. If I hadn't known better, I would have sworn he had no eyeballs, only two black, empty spaces.

"Oh, it's you," he said, voice low, lips hardly moving. "I thought I felt you searching for me." He craned over Mr Crepsley and looked down to where I was shaking. "I see you've brought the boy."

"May we come in?" Mr Crepsley asked.

"Of course. What is it one is supposed to say to you vampires?" He smiled. "Enter of your own free will?"

"Something like that," Mr Crepsley replied, and from the smile on his face, I knew it was an old joke between them.

We entered the van and sat. It was pretty bare inside, just a few shelves with posters and leaflets for the Cirque, the tall red hat and gloves I'd seen him wear before, a couple of knick-knacks and a foldaway bed.

"I didn't expect you back so soon, Larten," Mr Tall said. Even when he was sitting down he looked enormous.

"A swift return had not been on the agenda, Hibernius." *Hibernius?* That was a strange name. Still, it suited him somehow. Hibernius Tall. It had an odd ring to it.

"Did you run into trouble?" Mr Tall asked.

"No," Mr Crepsley said. "Darren was not happy. I decided he would be better off here, among those of his own kind."

"I see." Mr Tall studied me curiously. "You have come a long way since I saw you last, Darren Shan," he said.

"I preferred it where I was," I grumbled.

"Then why did you leave?" he asked.

I glared at him. "You know why," I said coldly.

He nodded slowly.

"Is it OK if we stay?" Mr Crepsley asked.

"Of course," Mr Tall replied immediately. "Delighted to have you back, actually. We're a bit under-staffed at the moment. Alexander Ribs, Sive and Seersa, and Gertha Teeth are off on holidays or business. Cormac Limbs is on his way to join us, but is late getting here. Larten Crepsley and his amazing performing spider will be an invaluable addition to the line-up."

"Thank you," Mr Crepsley said.

"What about me?" I asked boldly.

Mr Tall smiled. "You are less valuable," he said, "but welcome all the same."

I snorted, but said nothing.

"Where shall we be playing?" Mr Crepsley asked next.

"Right here," Mr Tall told him.

"*Here?*" I piped up in surprise.

"That puzzles you?" Mr Tall enquired.

"It's in the middle of nowhere," I said. "I thought you only played in towns and cities, where you'd get big audiences."

"We *always* get a big audience," Mr Tall said. "No matter where we play, people will come. Usually we stick to more populated areas, but this is a slow time of the year for us. As I've said, several of our best performers are absent, as are ... certain other members of our company."

A strange, secretive look passed between Mr Tall and Mr Crepsley, and I felt I was being left out of something.

"So we are resting for a while," Mr Tall went on. "We shall not be putting on any shows for a few days. We're relaxing."

"We passed a road-camp on our way," Mr Crepsley said. "Are they causing any problems?"

"The foot-soldiers of NOP?" Mr Tall laughed. "They're too busy defending trees and rocks to interfere with us."

"What's NOP?" I asked.

"Nature's Opposing Protectors," Mr Tall explained. "They're Eco Warriors. They run around the country, trying to stop new roads and bridges being built. They've been here a couple of months, but are due to move on soon."

"Are they real warriors?" I asked. "Do they have guns and grenades and tanks?"

The two adults almost laughed their heads off.

"He can be quite silly sometimes," Mr Crepsley said between fits of laughter, "but he is not as dumb as he seems."

I felt my face reddening, but held my tongue. I knew from experience that it's no use getting mad at grown-ups when they laugh at you; it only makes them laugh even harder.

"They call themselves warriors," Mr Tall said, "but they're not really. They chain themselves to trees and pour sand into the engines of JCBs and toss nails in the path of cars. That sort of thing."

"Why—" I started, but Mr Crepsley interrupted.

"We do not have time for questions," he said. "A few more minutes and the sun will be up." He rose and shook Mr Tall's hand. "Thank you for having us back, Hibernius."

"My pleasure," Mr Tall replied.

"I trust you took good care of my coffin?"

"Of course."

Mr Crepsley smiled happily and rubbed his hands together. "That is what I miss most when I am away. It will be nice to bed down in it once more."

"What about the boy?" Mr Tall asked. "Do you want us to knock together a coffin for him?"

"Don't even think about it!" I shouted. "You won't get me in one of those again!" I remembered what it felt like to be in a coffin, when I was buried alive, and shivered.

Mr Crepsley smiled. "Put Darren in with one of the other performers," he said. "Somebody his own age, if possible."

Mr Tall thought a moment. "How about Evra?"

Mr Crepsley's smile spread. "Yes. I think putting him in with Evra is a marvellous idea."

"Who's Evra?" I asked nervously.

"You will find out," Mr Crepsley promised, opening the door to the van. "I will leave you to Mr Tall. He will take care of you. I have to be away."

And then he was gone, off to find his beloved coffin.

I glanced over my shoulder and found Mr Tall standing directly behind me. I don't know how he crossed the room so quickly. I didn't even hear him moving to stand up.

"Shall we go?" he said.

I gulped and nodded.

He led the way through the camp-site. The morning was breaking and I saw a couple of lights coming on in a few of the caravans and tents. Mr Tall led me to an old grey tent, big enough for five or six people.

"Here are some blankets," he said, handing over a bunch of woolly sheets. "And a pillow." I don't know where he got them from – he hadn't had them when we left the van – but was too tired to ask. "You may sleep as late as you wish. I will come for you when you are awake and explain your duties. Evra will take care of you until then."

I lifted the flap of the tent and looked inside. It was too dark to see anything. "Who's Evra?" I asked, turning back to Mr Tall. But he was gone, having disappeared with his usual rapid, silent speed.

I sighed and entered, clutching the blankets to my chest. I let the flap fall back into place, then stood quietly inside, waiting for my eyes to adjust. I could hear someone breathing softly, and could make out a vague shape in a hammock in the darkness beyond the middle of the tent. I looked for somewhere to make my bed. I didn't want my tent-mate tripping over me when he was getting up.

I walked forward a few blind steps. Suddenly, something slithered towards me through the darkness. I stopped and stared ahead, wishing desperately that I could see (without the light of the stars or moon, even a vampire struggles to make things out).

"Hello?" I called softly. "Are you Evra? I'm Darren Shan. I'm your new—"

I stopped. The slithering noise had reached my feet. As I stood, rooted to the spot, something fleshy and slimy wrapped itself around my legs. I instantly knew what it was, but didn't dare look down until it had climbed more than halfway up my body. Finally, as its coils curled around my chest, I worked up the courage to lower my eyes and lock gazes with that of a long, thick, hissing ... *snake!*

CHAPTER EIGHT

I STOOD frozen with fear for more than an hour, staring into the snake's deathly cold eyes, waiting for it to strike.

Finally, with the light of the strong morning sun shining through the canvas of the tent, the sleeping shape in the hammock shifted, yawned, sat up and looked around.

It was the snake-boy and he got a shock when he saw me. He rocked back in the hammock and raised the covers, as though to protect himself. Then he saw the snake wrapped around me and breathed easily.

"Who are you?" he asked sharply. "What are you doing here?"

I shook my head slowly. I didn't dare speak in case the movement of my lungs caused the snake to strike.

"You'd better answer," he warned, "or I'll tell her to take your eyes out."

"I ... I ... I'm Duh–Darren Sh–Sh–Shan," I stuttered. "Mr Tuh–Tall told me to cuh–come in. He said I wuh–wuh–was to be your new ruhruh–ruh–roommate."

"Darren Shan?" The snake-boy frowned, then pointed knowingly. "You're Mr Crepsley's assistant, aren't you?"

"Yes," I said quietly.

43

The snake-boy grinned. "Did he know Mr Tall was putting you in with me?" I nodded and he laughed. "I've never yet met a vampire without a nasty sense of humour."

He swung down out of the hammock, crossed the tent, took hold of the snake's head and began unwrapping it. "You're OK," he assured me. "In fact, you were never in danger. The snake's been asleep the whole time. You could have tugged her off and she wouldn't have stirred. She's a deep sleeper."

"She's *asleep*?" I squeaked. "But ... how come she wrapped herself around me?"

He smiled. "She sleep-crawls."

"*Sleep-crawls!*" I stared at him, then at the snake, which hadn't moved while he was unwinding her. The last of her coils came free and I was able to step away to one side. My legs were stiff and full of pins and needles.

"A sleep-crawling snake." I laughed uneasily. "Good job she's not a sleep-*eating* snake!"

The snake-boy tucked his pet away in a corner and stroked her head lovingly. "She wouldn't have eaten you even if she had woken up," he informed me. "She ate a goat yesterday. Snakes her size don't have to eat very often."

Leaving his snake, he threw back the tent-flap and stepped out. I followed quickly, not wanting to be left alone with the reptile.

I studied him closely outside. He was exactly as I remembered: a few years older than me, very thin with long yellow-green hair, narrow eyes, strangely webbed fingers and toes; his body was covered in scales of green, gold, yellow and blue. He was wearing a pair of shorts and nothing else.

"By the way," he said, "my name's Evra Von." He held out a hand and we shook. His palm felt slippery, but dry. A few of the scales came off and stuck to my hand when I pulled it away. They were like scraps of coloured dead skin.

"Evra Von what?" I asked.

"Just plain Von," he said, rubbing his stomach. "You hungry?"

"Yes," I said, and went with Evra to get something to eat.

The camp was alive with activity. Since there had been no show the night before, most of the freaks and their helpers had gone to bed early, and so were up and about earlier than usual.

I was fascinated by the hustle and bustle. I hadn't realized there were so many people working for the Cirque. I'd thought it would just be the performers and assistants I'd seen the night I went to the show with Steve, but as I looked around I saw that those were just the tip of the iceberg. There were at least two dozen people walking or talking, washing or cooking, none of whom I'd seen before.

"Who are all these?" I asked.

"The backbone of the Cirque Du Freak," Evra replied. "They do the driving, set up the tents, the laundry, the cooking, mend our costumes, clear up after shows. It's a big operation."

"Are they normal humans?" I asked.

"Most of them," he said.

"How did they come to work here?"

"Some are related to the performers. Some are friends of Mr Tall. Some just wandered in, liked what they saw and stayed."

"People can do that?" I asked.

"If Mr Tall likes the look of them," Evra said. "There are always vacancies at the Cirque Du Freak."

Evra stopped at a large camp-fire and I stopped beside him. Hans Hands (a man who could walk on his hands and run faster on them than the world's fastest sprinter) was resting on a log, while Truska (the Bearded Lady, who grew her beard whenever she wanted) cooked sausages on a wooden stick. Several humans were sitting or lying about.

"Morning greetings, Evra Von," Hans Hands said.

"How do, Hans," Evra replied.

"Who's your young friend?" Hans asked, eyeing me suspiciously.

"This is Darren Shan," Evra said.

"*The* Darren Shan?" Hans asked, eyebrows raising.

"None other," Evra grinned.

"What do you mean ... '*The* Darren Shan'?" I asked.

"You're famous round these parts," Hans said.

"Why? Because I'm a –" I lowered my voice "– half-vampire?"

Hans laughed pleasantly. "Half-vampires are nothing new. If I had a gold coin for every half-vampire I'd seen, I'd have ..." He scrunched up his face and thought. "Twenty-nine gold coins. But *young* half-vampires are a different matter. I never saw or heard of a boy your age living it up amongst the ranks of the walking dead. Tell me: have the Vampire Generals been round to inspect you yet?"

"Who are the Vampire Generals?" I asked.

"They're—"

"Hans!" a lady washing clothes barked. He stopped speaking and looked around guiltily. "Do you think Larten would enjoy hearing you spreading tales?" she snapped.

Hans pulled a face. "Sorry," he said. "It's the fresh morning air. I'm not used to it. Makes me say things I shouldn't."

I wanted him to explain about the Vampire Generals, but it would have been impolite to ask.

Truska checked the sausages, pulled a couple off the stick and handed them out. She smiled when she came to me and said something in a strange, foreign language.

Evra laughed. "She wants to know if you like sausages or if you're a vegetarian."

"That's a good one!" Hans chuckled. "A vampire vegetarian!"

46

"You speak her language?" I asked Evra.

"Yes," he said proudly. "I'm still learning — it's the hardest language I've ever tried to learn — but I'm the only one in the camp who knows what she's saying. I'm excellent at languages," he boasted.

"What language is it?" I asked.

"I don't know," he said, frowning. "She won't tell me."

That sounded odd, but I didn't want to say anything to offend him. Instead, I took one of the sausages and smiled my thanks. I bit into it and had to let go straight away; it was roasting hot! Evra laughed and handed me a mug of water. I drank until my mouth was back to normal, then blew on the sausage to cool it down.

We sat with Hans and Truska and the others for a while, chatting and eating and soaking up the morning sun. The grass was damp with dew, but none of us minded. Evra introduced me to everyone in the group. There were too many names for me to memorize in one go, so I just smiled, shook hands and filed the faces away.

Mr Tall appeared before long. One moment he wasn't there, the next he was standing behind Evra, warming his hands over the fire.

"You're up early, Master Shan," Mr Tall remarked.

"I couldn't sleep," I told him. "I was too —" I looked over at Evra and smiled "— wound-up."

"I hope it will not affect your ability to work," Mr Tall said.

"I'll be fine," I said. "I'm ready and able."

"You're sure?"

"I'm sure."

"That's what I like to hear." He produced a large notebook and flipped through the pages. "Let's see what we can find for you to do today," he mused. "Tell me: are you a good cook?"

"I can cook a stew. Mr Crepsley taught me."

"Have you ever cooked for a company of thirty or forty?"

"No."

"Too bad. Maybe you'll learn." He flicked through another couple of pages. "Can you sew and stitch?"

"No."

"Have you washed clothes before?"

"By hand?"

"Yes."

"No."

"Hurm." He flicked on some more, then snapped the book shut. "OK," he said, "until we find a more permanent position for you, stick with Evra and help him with his chores. Does that sound fair?"

"I'd like that," I said.

"You don't mind, Evra?" he asked the snake-boy.

"Not at all," Evra replied.

"Very well. It's settled. Evra will be in charge of you until further notice. Do what he says. When your colleague-in-blood arises —" he meant Mr Crepsley "— you're free to spend the night with him if he so desires. We'll see how you get on, then make a decision on how best to utilize your talents."

"Thank you," I said.

"My pleasure," he replied.

I expected him to vanish in the blink of an eye then, but instead he turned and walked away slowly, whistling, enjoying the sunshine.

"Well, Darren," Evra said, sticking a scaly arm around my shoulders, "looks like you and me are partners now. How do you feel about that?"

"I feel good ... partner."

"Excellent!" He clapped my shoulder and gulped down the

last of his sausage. "Then let's get busy."

"What do we do first?" I asked.

"What we'll be doing first every morning," Evra said, setting off. "Milking the poison from the fangs of my snake."

"Oh," I said, coming to a halt. "Is it dangerous?"

"Only if she bites before we finish," Evra said, then laughed at my expression and pushed me ahead of him to the tent.

CHAPTER NINE

EVRA DID the milking himself — to my great relief — then we dragged the snake outside and laid her on the grass. We fetched buckets of water and scrubbed her down with very soft sponges.

After that, we had to feed the Wolf Man. His cage was near the back of the camp-site. He roared when he saw us coming. He looked as angry and dangerous as he had that night I visited the Cirque with Steve. He shook the bars and swiped at us if we got too close — which we didn't!

"Why is he so vicious?" I asked, tossing him a large chunk of raw meat, which he grabbed in mid-air and bit into.

"Because he's a real Wolf Man," Evra said. "He's not just somebody very hairy. He's half-human, half-wolf."

"Isn't it cruel to keep him chained up?" I asked, throwing him another slice of meat.

"If we didn't, he'd run riot and kill people. The mix of human and wolf blood has driven him mad. He wouldn't just kill when he was hungry; if he was free, he'd murder all the time."

"Isn't there a cure?" I asked, feeling sorry for him.

"There isn't a cure because it isn't a disease," Evra explained.

"This isn't something he caught, it's how he was born. This is what he is."

"How did it happen?" I asked.

Evra looked at me seriously. "Do you really want to know?"

I stared at the hairy beast in the cage, ripping up the meat as if it was candy-floss, then gulped and said, "No, I suppose I don't."

We handled a variety of jobs after that. We peeled potatoes for that night's dinner, helped repair a tyre on one of the cars, spent an hour painting the roof of a van and walked a dog. Evra said most days were like this, just wandering through the camp, seeing what needed doing, helping out as and when required.

In the evening we took a load of cans and broken bits of glass to the tent of Rhamus Twobellies, a huge man who could eat anything. I wanted to stay and watch him eat, but Evra hurried me out. Rhamus didn't like people watching him eat in private.

We had a lot of time to ourselves, and during our quieter moments we told each other about our lives, where we'd come from and how we'd grown up.

Evra had been born to ordinary parents. They'd been horrified when they saw him. They abandoned him at an orphanage, where he stayed until a nasty circus owner bought him at the age of four.

"Those were bad days," he said quietly. "He used to beat me and treat me like a real snake. He kept me locked up in a glass cage and let people pay to look and laugh at me."

He'd been with the circus for seven long, miserable years, touring small towns, being made to feel ugly and freakish and useless.

Finally, Mr Tall came to the rescue.

"He turned up one night," Evra said. "He appeared suddenly, out of the darkness, and stood by my cage for a long time, watching me. He didn't say a word. Neither did I.

"The circus owner came. He didn't know who Mr Tall was, but thought he might be a rich man, interested in buying me. He stated his price and stood back, waiting for an answer.

"Mr Tall didn't say anything for a few minutes. Then his left hand grabbed the circus owner by the neck. He squeezed once and that was the end of him. He fell to the floor, dead. Mr Tall opened the door to my cage and said, "Let's go, Evra." I think Mr Tall's able to read minds, which is how he knew my name."

Evra was quiet after that. He had a faraway look in his eyes.

"Do you want to see something amazing?" he said eventually, snapping out of his thoughtful mood.

"Sure," I said.

He turned to face me, then stuck out his tongue and pushed it up over his lip and *right up his nose!*

"Ewww! Gross!" I yelled delightedly.

He pulled the tongue back and grinned. "I've got the longest tongue in the world," he said. "If my nose was big enough, I could poke my tongue all the way to the top, down my throat and back out my mouth again."

"You couldn't!" I laughed.

"Probably not," he giggled. "But it's still pretty impressive." He ran the tongue out again and this time licked around his nostrils, one after the other. It was revolting but hilarious.

"That's the most disgusting thing I've ever seen," I laughed.

"I bet you wish you could do it," Evra said.

"I wouldn't, even if I could," I lied. "Don't you get snot all over your tongue?"

"I don't have any snot," Evra said.

"What? No snot?"

"It's true," he said. "My nose is different to yours. There's no snot or dirt or hairs. My nostrils are the cleanest part of my whole body."

"What does it taste like?" I asked.

"Lick my snake's belly and you'll find out," he replied. "It's the same taste as that."

I laughed and said I wasn't *that* interested!

Later, when Mr Crepsley asked me what I'd done all day, I replied simply: "I made a friend."

CHAPTER TEN

WE'D BEEN with the Cirque two days and nights. I spent my days with Evra, helping him, and my nights with Mr Crepsley, learning about vampires. I was going to bed earlier than I had been, though I rarely hit the sack before one or two in the morning.

I'd struck up a strong friendship with Evra. He was older than me, but he was shy — probably because of his troubled past — so we were pretty well suited.

As the third day rolled by, I found myself gazing around the small groups of vans and cars and tents, feeling like I'd been part of the scene for years.

I was starting to suffer from the effects of going so long without drinking human blood. I wasn't as strong as I had been, and couldn't move as quickly as I could before. My eyesight had dulled, as had my hearing and sense of smell. I was much stronger and quicker than I'd been as a human, but I could feel my powers slipping, a bit more every day.

I didn't mind. I'd rather lose some strength than drink from a human.

I was relaxing with Evra on the edge of the camp-site that

afternoon when we spotted a figure in the bushes.

"Who's that?" I asked.

"A kid from a nearby village," Evra said. "I've seen him hanging around before."

I watched the boy in the bushes. He was trying hard not to be seen, but to a person with my powers — fading though they were — he was as obvious as an elephant. I was curious to know what he was doing, so I turned to Evra and said, "Let's have fun."

"What are you planning?" he asked.

"Lean in and I'll tell you."

I whispered my plan in his ear. He grinned and nodded, then stood and pretended to yawn.

"I'll be off, Darren," he said. "See you later."

"See you, Evra," I replied loudly. I waited until he was gone, then stood and walked back to the camp myself.

When I was out of sight of the boy in the bushes, I doubled back, using the caravans and tents to mask my movements. I walked about a hundred metres to the left, then crept forward until I was level with the boy, and sneaked towards him.

I stopped ten metres away. I was a little bit behind him, so he couldn't see me. His eyes were still glued to the camp. I looked over his head and saw Evra, who was even closer than I was. He made an "OK" sign with his thumb and index finger.

I crouched down low and moaned.

"Ohhhh," I groaned. "Wwwooohhhh."

The boy stiffened and looked over his shoulder nervously. He wasn't able to see me.

"Who's there?" he asked.

"Wraaarghhhh," Evra grunted on the other side of him.

The boy's head spun around in the other direction.

"Who's there?" he shouted.

"Ohh-ohh-ohh," I snorted, in the manner of a gorilla.

"I'm not afraid," the boy said, edging backwards. "You're just somebody playing a nasty trick."

"Eee-ee-ee-ee-ee," Evra screeched.

I shook a branch, Evra rattled a bush, then I tossed a stone into the area just ahead of the boy. His head was spinning round like a puppet's, darting all over the place. He didn't know whether it would be safer to run or stay.

"Look, I don't know who you are," he began, "but I'm—"

Evra had sneaked up behind him and now, as the boy spoke, stuck out his extra-long tongue and ran it over the boy's neck, making a hissing snake noise.

That was enough for the boy. He screamed and ran for his life.

Evra and me ran after him, laughing our socks off, making noises all the time. He fled through thorn bushes and nettles as though they weren't there, screaming for help.

We grew tired of the game after a few minutes, and might have let him get away, but then he tripped and went sprawling into a patch of very high grass.

We stood, trying to spot him amongst the grass, but there was no sign of him.

"Where is he?" I asked.

"I can't see him," Evra said.

"Do you think he's all right?"

"I don't know." Evra looked worried. "He might have fallen down a big hole or something."

"Kid?" I shouted. "Are you OK?" No answer. "There's no need to be afraid. We won't hurt you. We were only fooling. We didn't—"

There was a rushing noise behind us, then I felt a hand on my back, shoving me forward into the grass. Evra fell with me and, when we sat up, spluttering with shock, we heard somebody laughing behind us.

We turned slowly, and there was the kid, bent over double with laughter.

"Fooled you! Fooled you!" he sang, dancing about. "I saw you coming from the beginning. I was only pretending to be frightened. I ambushed you. Ha-ha. Ohh-ohh-ohh. Eee-ee-ee."

He was making fun of us and, though we felt pretty foolish, when we stood and looked at each other we burst out laughing. He'd led us into a patch of grass filled with sticky green seeds and we were covered in them from head to foot.

"You look like a walking plant," I joked.

"*You* look like the Jolly Green Giant," Evra replied.

"Both of you look stupid," the boy said. We stared at him and his smile faded a bit. "Well, you *do*," he grumbled.

"I suppose you think this is funny," I snarled. He nodded silently. "Well, I've got news for you, kid," I said, stepping closer, putting on the meanest face I could. I paused menacingly, then burst into a smile. "It is!"

He laughed happily, relieved that we could see the sunny side of things, then stuck out his hands, one to either of us. "Hi," he said as we shook. "My name's Sam Grest. Pleased to meetcha."

"Hi, Sam Grest," I said, and as I shook his hand, I thought to myself, "Looks like this is friend number two."

And he did become my friend. But by the time the Cirque Du Freak moved on, I was wishing with all my heart that I'd never even heard his name.

CHAPTER ELEVEN

SAM LIVED about a kilometre away, with his mum and dad, two younger brothers and a baby sister, three dogs, five cats, two budgies, a turtle, and a tank full of tropical fish.

"It's like living in Noah's Ark," he laughed. "I try and stay out of the house as much as possible. Mum and Dad don't mind. They think children should be free to express their individuality. As long as I turn up for bed at night, they're happy. They don't even care if I miss school every once in a while. They think school's a despotic system of indoctrination, designed to crush the spirit and stamp out creativity."

Sam talked like that all the time. He was younger than me, but you wouldn't have known it by listening to him speak.

"So, you two guys are with the show?" he asked, rolling a piece of pickled onion around his mouth – he loved pickled onions and carried a small plastic jar of them with him. We'd returned to the spot at the edge of the clearing. Evra was lying in the grass, I was sitting on a low-hanging branch, Sam was climbing the tree above me.

"What sort of a show is it?" he asked, before we could answer his first question. "There are very few markings on the vans. At first I thought you were travellers. Then, after observing for a while, I decided you must be performers of one sort or another."

"We're masters of the macabre," Evra said. "Agents of mutations. Lords of the surreal." He was speaking like that to show he could match Sam's fancy way with the language. I wish I could have spouted a few grand-sounding sentences, but I'd never been good with words.

"It's a magic show?" Sam asked excitedly.

"It's a freak show," I said.

"A *freak* show?" His jaw dropped open and the bit of pickled onion fell out. I had to move quickly to dodge it. "Two-headed men and anomalies such as that?"

"Sort of," I said, "but our performers are magical, wonderful artists, not just people who look different."

"Cool!" He glanced at Evra. "Of course, I could see from the start that you were dermatologically challenged — " he was talking about Evra's skin (I looked the word up in a dictionary later) "—but I'd no idea there might be other members like you among your company."

He looked over towards the camp, eyes alight with curiosity. "This is most fascinating," he sighed. "What other bizarre examples of the human form do your numbers hoard?"

"If you mean, 'What other sort of performers are there?', the answer is loads," I told him. "We have a bearded lady, of course."

"A Wolf Man," Evra said.

"A man with two bellies," I added.

We went through the entire list, Evra mentioning some I'd never seen. The line-up of the Cirque Du Freak often changed. Performers came and went, depending on where the show was playing.

Sam was greatly impressed and, for the first time since we'd met, had nothing to say. He listened silently, eyes wide, sucking on one of his pickled onions, shaking his head every so often as though he couldn't believe what he was hearing.

"It's incredible," he said softly when we finished. "You must be the luckiest kids on the planet. Living with real circus freaks, travelling the world, privy to solemn and magnificent secrets. What I wouldn't give to trade places with you ..."

I smiled to myself. I don't think he'd have liked to trade places with *me*, not if he knew my full story.

"Hey!" he said, a thought striking him. "I don't suppose you could swing it for me to join? I'm a hard worker, bright as a button, used to responsibility. I'd be an asset. Could I join? As an assistant? Please?"

Evra and me smiled at each other.

"I don't think so, Sam," Evra said. "We don't take on many kids. If you were older, or if your parents wanted to join, that would be different."

"But they wouldn't mind," Sam insisted. "They'd be delighted for me. They're always saying travel broadens the mind. They'd love the idea of me going around the world, having adventures, seeing marvellous, mystical sights."

Evra shook his head. "Sorry. Maybe when you're older."

Sam pouted and kicked some leaves off a nearby branch. They floated down over me and a couple stuck in my hair.

"It's not fair," Sam grumbled. "People always say 'when you're older'. Where would the world be if Alexander the Great had 'waited until he was older'? And how about Joan of Arc? If she'd 'waited until she was older', the English might have conquered and colonized France. Who decides when someone's old enough to make decisions for themselves? It should be down to the individual."

He ranted on for a while longer, complaining about adults and the "corrupt, bloody system" and about the time being ripe for a children's revolution. It was like listening to a crazy politician on television.

"If a child wants to open a chocolate factory, let him open one," Sam stormed. "If he wants to become a jockey, fine. If he wants to be an explorer and set off for strange, cannibal-populated islands, OK! We're the slaves of the modern generation. We're—"

"Sam," Evra interrupted. "Do you want to come see my snake?"

Sam broke out into a smile. "Do I!" he yelled. "I thought you'd never ask. C'mon, let's go." Leaping down out of the tree, he set off for the camp-site at top speed, speeches forgotten. We followed slowly, laughing gently, feeling much older and wiser than we were.

CHAPTER TWELVE

SAM THOUGHT the snake was the coolest thing he'd ever seen. He wasn't a bit scared, and didn't hesitate to wrap her around his neck like a scarf. He asked all sorts of questions: how long was she, what did she eat, how often did she shed her skin, where was she from, what type of snake was she, how fast could she move?

Evra answered all of Sam's questions. He was a snake expert. There wasn't a thing he didn't know about the serpent kingdom. He was even able to tell Sam roughly how many scales the snake had!

We gave Sam a guided tour of the camp-site after that. We took him to see the Wolf Man (Sam was very quiet in the shade of the hairy Wolf Man's van, frightened by the snarling creature within). We introduced him to Hans Hands. Then we chanced upon Rhamus Twobellies practising his act. Evra asked if we could watch and Rhamus let us. Sam's eyes almost popped out of his head when he saw Rhamus chew a cup into tiny pieces, swallow it, piece it back together inside his belly and bring it up his throat and out his mouth.

I was going to fetch Madam Octa and show Sam some of the tricks I could do with her, but I didn't feel too hot. The lack of human blood in my diet was getting to me; my belly often grumbled hungrily, no matter how much food I ate, and I sometimes got sick or had to sit down suddenly. I didn't want to faint or get sick with the spider out of her cage; I knew from experience how deadly she could be if you lost control of her for even a couple of seconds.

Sam would have stayed for ever, but it was getting dark and I knew Mr Crepsley would be waking soon. Evra and me had jobs to do, so we told him it was time he went home.

"Can't I stay a while longer?" he pleaded.

"Your dinner will be ready," Evra said.

"I can eat with you," Sam said.

"There isn't enough food," I lied.

"Well, I'm not very hungry anyway," Sam said. "It's amazing how filling pickled onions can be."

"Maybe he could stay," Evra mused. I stared at him, surprised, but he winked to show he was only pretending.

"Could I?" Sam asked, delighted.

"Sure," Evra said. "But you'll have to help us with our jobs."

"I'll do anything," Sam said. "I don't mind. What is it?"

"The Wolf Man needs feeding and washing and brushing," Evra said.

Sam's smile slipped.

"The wuh—wolf—muh—man?" he asked nervously.

"It's no problem," Evra told him. "He's normally quiet once he's been fed. He hardly ever bites his helpers. If he *does* attack, keep your head clear of his mouth and stick an arm down his throat. It's better to lose an arm than your—"

"You know," Sam said quickly, "I think I *do* have to go home. Mum said something about friends coming over tonight."

"Oh. That's a pity." Evra grinned.

Sam backed away, gazing in the direction of the Wolf Man's

cage. He looked sad to be going, so I called for him to stop.

"What are you doing tomorrow?" I asked.

"Nothing," he said.

"Do you want to come over in the afternoon and hang out with us?"

"You bet!" Sam whooped, then paused. "I won't have to help feed and clean the ...?" He gulped loudly.

"No," Evra said, still smiling.

"Then I'll be here. See you tomorrow, guys."

"See you, Sam," we said together.

He waved, turned and departed.

"Sam's nice, isn't he?" I said to Evra.

"A good kid," Evra agreed. "He could do with not trying to sound so smart all the time, and he's a bit of a scaredy-cat, but otherwise there's nothing wrong with him."

"Do you think he'd fit in if he did join the show?" I asked.

Evra snorted. "Like a mouse in a house full of cats!"

"What do you mean?" I asked.

"This life isn't for everyone. A few weeks away from his family, having to clean out toilets and cook for thirty or forty people ... He'd be running screaming for the hills."

"*We* manage all right," I said.

"We're different," Evra said. "We're not like other people. This is what we're cut out for. Everybody has a place where they belong. This is ours. We're meant to ..."

He stopped and began to frown. He was glancing over my head at something in the distance. I turned to see what was bothering him. For a few seconds I couldn't make out anything, but then, some way off, coming through the trees to the east, I glimpsed the flickering light of a burning torch.

"Who could that be?" I asked.

"I'm not sure," Evra said.

We watched for a few minutes as the torch came closer. I saw figures moving beneath the cover of the trees. I couldn't tell how many there were, but it had to be at least six or seven. Then, as they broke free of the trees, I saw who they were, and goosebumps sprang to life along my neck and arms.

The walkers were the small blue-hooded people that Steve and me had seen the night of the show, the ones who helped sell sweets and toys to the crowd, and assisted with the acts. I'd forgotten about those strange blue-hooded helpers. It had been several months since that night, and I'd had other things on my mind.

They came out of the woods in pairs, one set after the other. I counted twelve in all, though there was a thirteenth member, a taller person walking behind the rest. He was the one shining the torch.

"Where did they come from?" I asked Evra quietly.

"I don't know," he answered. "They left the show a few weeks ago. I've no idea where they went. They keep to themselves mostly."

"Who are they?" I asked.

"They're—" he began to answer, but stopped all of a sudden. His eyes widened with fear.

It was the man bringing up the rear, the thirteenth, taller member of the group – visible now that he was closer – who had scared Evra.

The blue-hooded people passed by silently. As the mysterious thirteenth person approached, I noticed he was dressed differently to the others. He wasn't very tall; he just looked big in comparison to the blue-hoods. He had short white hair, a thick pair of glasses, a sharp yellow suit and long green Wellington boots. He was quite plump and walked with a peculiar little waddle.

He smiled pleasantly at us as he passed. I smiled back but

Evra was rooted to the spot, unable to move the muscles of his mouth.

The blue-hoods and the man with the torch walked further into the camp-site, all the way to the back, where they found a large clear spot. There, the blue-hoods began putting up a tent – they must have been carrying the materials beneath their cloaks – while the larger man headed for Mr Tall's van.

I studied Evra. He was shaking all over and, though his face could never turn white – because of its natural colour – it was paler than it had ever been before.

"What's wrong?" I asked.

He shook his head silently, unable to reply.

"What is it? Why are you so frightened? Who was that man?"

"He ... It ..." Evra cleared his throat and took a deep breath. When he spoke, it was in a low, trembling voice, filled with sheer, blood-chilled terror.

"That was *Mr Tiny*," he said, and I could get no more out of him for ages after that.

CHAPTER THIRTEEN

EVRA'S FEAR faded as evening wore on, but he was very slow to return to normal and was uncommonly edgy the whole night long. I had to take his knife from him and do his share when he was peeling potatoes for the dinner; I was afraid he might slice one of his fingers off.

After we'd eaten and helped wash up, I asked Evra about the mysterious Mr Tiny. We were in the tent and Evra was playing with his snake.

He didn't reply immediately, and for a while I thought he wasn't going to, but in the end he sighed and began to speak.

"Mr Tiny is the leader of the Little People," he said.

"The small guys in the blue-hooded cloaks?" I asked.

"Yes. He calls them Little People. He's their boss. He doesn't come here often – it's been two years since I last saw him – but he gives me the creeps when he does. He's the spookiest man I've ever met."

"He looked all right to me," I said.

"That's what I thought the first time I saw him," Evra agreed. "But wait until you've spoken to him. It's hard to explain, but every time he looks at me, I feel like he's planning to slaughter, skin and roast me."

"He eats people?" I asked, aghast.

"I don't know," Evra said. "Maybe he does, maybe he doesn't. But you get the feeling he *wants* to eat you. And it's not just me being silly; I've discussed it with other members of the Cirque and they feel the same way. Nobody likes him. Even Mr Tall gets fidgety when Mr Tiny's around."

"Well, the Little People must like him, mustn't they?" I asked. "They follow and obey him, don't they?"

"Maybe they're scared of him," Evra said. "Maybe he forces them to obey him. Perhaps they're his slaves."

"Have you ever asked them?"

"They don't talk," Evra said. "I don't know if it's because they can't or they prefer not to, but nobody in the circus has ever been able to get a word out of them. They're very helpful and they'll do whatever you ask but they're as silent as walking dummies."

"Have you ever seen their faces?" I asked.

"Once," Evra said. "Normally they don't let their hoods slip, but one day I was helping a couple of them move a heavy machine. It fell on one of the Little People and crushed him. He didn't make a sound, even though he must have been in a huge amount of pain. His hood fell to the side and I caught a glimpse of his face.

"It was horrible," Evra said quietly, stroking his snake softly. "Full of scars and stitches and crumpled in on itself, as though some giant had squeezed it with his claws. It had no ears or nose, and there was some sort of a mask over its mouth. The skin was grey and dead-looking, and his eyes were like two green bowls near the top of his face. He had no hair."

Evra shivered at the memory. I felt cold myself, thinking about his description.

"What happened to him?" I asked. "Did he die?"

"I don't know," Evra said. "A couple of his brothers – I always think of them as brothers, though they probably aren't — turned up and carted him away."

"You never saw him again?"

"They all look the same," Evra said. "Some are a bit smaller or taller than the rest, but there's no real way of telling them apart. Believe me: I've tried."

Stranger and stranger. I was really interested in Mr Tiny and his Little People. I'd always liked mysteries. Perhaps I could solve this one. Maybe, with my vampire powers, I could find a way to talk with one of the hooded creatures.

"Where do the Little People come from?" I asked.

"Nobody knows," Evra said. "There's usually four or six of them with the Cirque. Sometimes more turn up by themselves. Sometimes Mr Tiny brings new ones in. It was odd that none were here when you arrived."

"You think it had something to do with me and Mr Crepsley coming?" I asked.

"I doubt it," Evra said. "It was probably just coincidence. Or fate." He paused. "Which is another thing: Mr Tiny's first name is Desmond."

"So?"

"He tells people to call him Des."

"So?" I asked again.

"Put it together with his surname," Evra told me.

I did. Mr Des Tiny. Mr Des-Tiny. Mr ...

"*Mr Destiny*," I whispered, and Evra nodded seriously.

I was bursting with curiosity and asked Evra many more questions, but his answers were limited. He knew almost nothing of Mr Tiny, and only slightly more of the Little People. They ate meat. They smelled funny. They moved slowly most of the time. They either didn't feel pain or couldn't show it. And they had no sense of humour.

"How do you know that?" I asked.

"Bradley Stretch," Evra answered darkly. "He used to be with the show. He had rubbery bones and could make his arms and legs stretch.

"He wasn't very nice. He was constantly playing practical jokes on us and he had a nasty way of laughing. He didn't just make you look like a fool: he made you feel like one too.

"We played a show in an Arabian palace. It was a private show for a sheikh. He enjoyed all the acts but especially liked Bradley's. The two got chatting and Bradley told the sheikh he couldn't wear jewellery, because it always slipped off or burst, because of the changing shape of his body.

"The sheikh hurried away and came back with a small gold bracelet. He gave it to Bradley and told him to put it on his wrist. Bradley did. Then the sheikh told him to try shaking it off.

"Well, Bradley made his arm small and big, short and long, but he couldn't shake that bracelet loose. The sheikh said it was magic and could only be removed if the wearer wanted to take it off. It was very valuable, priceless, but he made Bradley a gift of it, to show his appreciation.

"Getting back to the Little People," Evra said. "Bradley loved to tease them. He was always finding new ways to trick them. He fixed traps to hang them up in the air by their feet. He set their cloaks on fire. He squirted washing-up liquid on ropes they were using, to make their hands slip, or glue to make them stick. He put thumb-tacks in their food, he made their tent collapse, he locked them into a van."

"Why was he so mean?" I asked.

"I think because they never reacted," Evra said. "He liked to see people get upset but the Little People never cried or screamed or lashed out. They seemed to take no notice of his pranks. At least, everybody *thought* they took no notice ..."

Evra made a funny noise that was half a laugh, half a moan. "One morning we woke up and Bradley had disappeared. Nowhere to be found. We searched for him, but when he didn't turn up, we moved on. We weren't worried; performers join and leave the Cirque pretty much as they please. It wasn't the first time one had sneaked away in the middle of the night.

"I thought no more about it until a week or so later. Mr Tiny had been to see us the day before and taken all but two of the Little People with him. Mr Tall told me I had to help the remaining pair with their duties. I tidied around their tent and rolled up their hammocks – they all sleep in hammocks. That's where I got mine from. Did I mention that before?"

He hadn't, but I didn't want to side-track him, so I said nothing.

"After that," he went on, "I gave their pot a wash. It was a big black pot, set on a fire in the middle of the tent. The place must have been full of smoke whenever they cooked, and the pot was covered in grime.

"I took it outside and emptied the remains of their last few meals – scraps of meat and bits of bone – on to the grass. I scrubbed it thoroughly, then took it back inside. Next I decided to gather up the bits of meat in the grass and throw them to the Wolf Man. 'Waste not, want not', as Mr Tall often says.

"As I was gathering up the meat and bone, I noticed something glistening ..."

Evra turned away and rooted through a bag underneath his hammock. When he faced me, he was holding a small gold bracelet. He let my eyes linger on it, then slipped it on over his left hand. He shook his arm as fast as he could but the bracelet never budged.

When he stopped shaking his arm, he slid the bracelet off with the fingers of his right hand and tossed it to me. I caught and examined it, but didn't put it on.

"The bracelet the sheikh gave to Bradley Stretch?" I guessed.

"The same," Evra said.

I handed it back.

"I don't know whether it was because of something especially bad he did," Evra said, fingering the bracelet, "or if they were just tired of the non-stop teasing. What I do know is, ever since, I've gone out of my way to be polite to the small silent people in the dark blue cloaks."

"What did you do with the remains of ... I mean, with the scraps of meat?" I asked. "Did you bury them?"

"Heck, no," Evra said. "I fed them to the Wolf Man, as I'd meant to." Then, in response to my horrified gasp, he said: 'Waste not, want not', remember?"

I stared at him in silence, then began to laugh. Evra chuckled too. In a minute we were rolling about on the floor, hugging our sides.

"We shouldn't laugh," I gasped. "Poor Bradley Stretch. We should be crying."

"I'm laughing too hard to cry," Evra giggled.

"I wonder what he tasted like?"

"I don't know," Evra said. "But I bet he was rubbery."

That made us laugh so much, tears rolled from our eyes and trickled down our cheeks. It was a terrible thing to laugh at, but we couldn't help ourselves.

In the middle of our fit of laughter, the flap to the door of our tent was poked aside by an inquisitive head and Hans Hands entered. "What's the joke?" he asked, but we couldn't tell him. I tried, but every time I started, I began laughing again.

He shook his head and smiled at our foolishness. Then, when we'd quietened down, he told us why he was here.

"I've a message for you two," he said. "Mr Tall wants you to report to his van as soon as possible."

"What's up, Hans?" Evra asked. He was still giggling. "Why does he want us?"

"He doesn't," Hans said. "Mr Tiny is with him. *He's* the one who wants you."

Our laughter stopped instantly. Hans let himself out without any further words.

"Mr Tuh-tuh-tuh-Tiny wants us," Evra gasped.

"I heard," I said. "What do you think he wants?"

"I don't kn–kn–kn–know," Evra stuttered, though I could see what was going through his mind. It was the same thing that was rushing through mine. We were thinking of the Little People, Bradley Stretch, and a big black pot full of scraps of human meat and bone.

CHAPTER FOURTEEN

MR TALL, Mr Crepsley and Mr Tiny were in the van when we entered. Evra was shaking like a leaf but I wasn't especially nervous. Mind you, when I saw the worried looks of Mr Tall and Mr Crepsley, and realized how uneasy they were, it set me on edge a little.

"Come in, boys," Mr Tiny welcomed us as though it was his van and not Mr Tall's. "Sit down, make yourselves at home."

"I'll stand, if it's all the same," Evra said, trying not to let us hear the chatter of his teeth.

"I'll stand too," I said, following Evra's lead.

"As you please," Mr Tiny said. He was the only one sitting.

"I've been hearing a lot about you, young Darren Shan," Mr Tiny said. He was rolling something between his hands: a heart-shaped watch. I could hear it ticking whenever there was a pause in his speech.

"You're quite the lad, by all accounts," Mr Tiny went on. "A most remarkable young man. Sacrificed everything to save a friend. There aren't many would do as much. People are so self-centred these days. It's great to see the world can still produce heroes."

"I'm no hero," I said, blushing at the compliment.

"Of course you are," he insisted. "What is a hero but a person who lays everything on the line for the good of somebody else?"

I smiled proudly. I couldn't understand why Evra was so afraid of this nice, odd man. There was nothing terrible about Mr Tiny. I quite liked him.

"Larten tells me you're reluctant to drink human blood," Mr Tiny said. "I don't blame you. Nasty, repulsive stuff. Can't stand it. Apart from young children, of course. Their blood is scrumdiddlyumptious."

I frowned. "You can't drink blood from them," I said. "They're too small. If you took blood from a young child, you'd kill it."

His eyes widened and so did his smile.

"*So?*" he asked softly.

A chill ran down my spine. If he'd been joking, it would have been in very poor taste, but I could have overlooked it (hadn't I just been laughing about poor Bradley Stretch?). But I could tell from his expression that he was perfectly serious.

All of a sudden, I knew why this man was so feared. *He was evil.* Not just bad or nasty, but pure demonic evil. This was a man I could imagine killing thousands of people, just to hear them scream.

"You know," Mr Tiny said, "your face seems familiar. Have we met before, Darren Shan?"

I shook my head.

"Are you certain?" he asked. "You look *very* familiar."

"I ... would have ... remembered," I gasped.

"You can't always trust memory," Mr Tiny smiled. "It can be a deceptive monster. Still, no matter. Maybe I'm confusing you with somebody else."

By the way his lips twisted into a grin (how had I ever thought that was a nice smile?), I could see he didn't think that. But I was sure he was wrong. There's no way I'd have forgotten meeting a creature like this.

"Down to business," Mr Tiny said. His hands tightened on the heart-shaped watch and for a moment they seemed to glow and melt into its ticking face. I blinked and rubbed my eyes. When I looked again, the illusion – which it must have been – had passed.

"You boys saw me arrive with my Little People," Mr Tiny said. "They're new converts to my cause and are a bit unsure of the ropes. Normally I'd stick around and teach them how to get along, but I have business elsewhere. Still, they're smart and I'm sure they'll learn.

"However, while they're learning, I'd like it if you two fine, decent boys would help ease them into the swing of things. You won't have to do much. Mainly I want you to find food for them. They have such big appetites.

"How about it, boys? I've got the permission of your guardians." He nodded at Mr Tall and Mr Crepsley, who didn't seem happy about the arrangement, but looked resigned. "Will you help poor old Mr Tiny and his Little People?"

I glanced at Evra. I could see he didn't want to agree to the request, but he nodded his head anyway. I did likewise.

"Excellent!" Mr Tiny boomed. "Young Evra Von knows what my darlings like, I'm sure. If you have any problems, report to Hibernius and he'll sort you out."

Mr Tiny waved a hand to let us know we could leave. Evra began edging backwards immediately, but I held my ground.

"Excuse me," I said, summoning all my courage, "but why do you call them Little People?"

Mr Tiny looked around slowly. If he was surprised by my question, he didn't show it, though I could see the mouths of Mr

Tall and Mr Crepsley dropping.

"Because they're little," he explained pleasantly.

"I know that," I said. "But don't they have another name? A proper name? If somebody mentioned 'Little People' to me, I'd think they were talking about Elves or Leprechauns."

Mr Tiny smiled. "They *are* Elves and Leprechauns," he said. "All around the world, you will find legends and stories of small, magical people. Legends have to start somewhere. These legends started with my short, loyal friends."

"Are you telling me those dwarfs in blue cloaks are *Elves*?" I asked disbelievingly.

"No," he said. "Elves don't exist. Those dwarfs — as you so rudely put it — were seen, long ago, by ignorant people, who invented names for them: Elves or Fairies or Sprites. They made up stories about what they were and what they could do."

"What *can* they do?" I asked curiously.

Mr Tiny's smile slipped. "I'd heard you were quite the one for asking questions," he growled, "but nobody told me you were *this* nosy. Remember, Darren Shan: curiosity killed the cat."

"I'm not a cat," I said cheekily.

Mr Tiny leaned forward and his face darkened. "If you ask more questions," he hissed, "you might find yourself turned into one. Nothing in life is for ever, not even the human form."

The watch in his hands glowed again, red like a real heart, and I decided the time had come to take my leave.

"Go to bed now and get a good night's sleep," Mr Crepsley told me before I left. "There will be no lessons tonight."

"And rise early, boys," Mr Tiny added, waving goodbye. "My Little People are always hungry in the mornings. It's not wise to let their hunger go unattended. You never know what they might set their minds — and *teeth* — on if they go unfed for too long."

We hurried out the door and raced back to our tent, where we fell to the floor and listened to our hearts beating loudly.

"Are you crazy?" Evra asked when he could speak. "Talking to Mr Tiny like that, asking him questions, you must be mad!"

"Yes," I said, thinking back on the encounter, wondering where I'd got the nerve from. "I must be."

Evra shook his head in disgust. It was early, but we crawled into bed anyway, where we lay awake for ages, staring at the ceiling of the tent. When I finally dropped off to sleep I dreamt of Mr Tiny and his heart-shaped watch. Only, in my dreams, it wasn't a watch. It was a real human heart. *Mine*. And when he squeezed it ...

Agony.

CHAPTER FIFTEEN

WE ROSE early and went hunting for food for the Little People. We were tired and grumpy and it took time for us to come to life.

After a while I asked Evra what the Little People liked to eat.

"Meat," he replied. "Any kind of animal, they don't care."

"How many animals will we need to catch?" I asked.

"Well, there's twelve of them, but they don't eat a lot. I guess one rabbit or hedgehog between two of them. A larger animal — a fox or a dog — might do three or four."

"Can you eat hedgehogs?" I asked.

"The Little People can," Evra said. "They're not fussy. They'd eat rats and mice too, but we'd have to catch loads to feed so many, so they're not worth bothering with."

We took a sack each and hit off in different directions. Evra told me the meat didn't have to be fresh, so if I found a dead badger or squirrel, I could stick it in the bag and save some time.

I spotted a fox a couple of minutes into the hunt. It had a chicken in its mouth and was on its way home. I tracked it until the moment was right, then pounced on it from behind a bush and dragged it to the ground.

The dead chicken flew from its mouth and it turned, snarling, to bite me. Before it could attack, I moved swiftly, grabbed its neck and twisted sharply to the left. There was a loud crack and that was the end of the fox.

I chucked the chicken into the bag — a welcome bonus — but hung on to the fox for a few minutes. I needed blood, so I found a vein, made a small cut, and started sucking.

Part of me hated this — it seemed inhuman — but I reminded myself that I *wasn't* human any more. I was a half-vampire. This was how my kind acted. I'd felt bad killing foxes and rabbits and pigs and sheep the first few times. But I got used to it. I had to.

Could I get used to drinking human blood? That was the question. I hoped I could avoid feeding on humans, but by the way I was running out of energy, I knew eventually I'd have to ... or die!

I tossed the body of the fox into the bag, then continued hunting. I found a family of rabbits washing their ears in a nearby pond. I crept as close as I could, then struck without warning. They scattered in fear, but not before I'd got my sharp fingernails into three of the little ones.

I added them to the contents of the bag and decided that would do for this trip. The fox, chicken and rabbits should easily feed six or seven of the blue-hoods.

I met Evra back at camp. He'd found a dead dog and badger and was feeling pretty pleased with himself. "The easiest day's hunting I've ever had," he said. "Plus I found a field full of cows. We'll go there tonight and steal one. It'll keep the Little People going for a day or two at least."

"Won't the farmer who owns them notice?" I asked.

"There are dozens of them," Evra said. "By the time he gets round to counting them, we'll be long gone."

"But cows cost money," I said. "I don't mind killing wild

animals, but stealing from a farmer is different."

"We'll leave money for him," Evra sighed.

"Where will we get it?" I asked.

Evra smiled. "The one thing we're never short of at the Cirque Du Freak is money," he assured me.

Later, our chores completed, we teamed up with Sam again. He'd been waiting in the bushes for ages.

"Why didn't you come into the camp?" I asked.

"I didn't like to impose," he said. "Besides, I thought somebody might have let the Wolf Man out. He didn't seem too fond of me when I saw him yesterday."

"He's like that with everyone," Evra told him.

"Maybe," Sam said, "but I figure it's best not to take chances."

Sam was in a questioning mood. He'd obviously been thinking about us a lot since the day before.

"Don't you ever wear shoes?" he asked Evra.

"No," Evra said. "The soles of my feet are extra tough."

"What happens if you step on a thorn or a nail?" Sam asked.

Evra smiled, sat down and gave Sam his foot. "Try scratching it with a sharp twig," he said.

Sam broke off a branch and prodded Evra's sole. I looked on with interest. It was like trying to make a hole in tough leather.

"A sharp piece of glass might slice me," Evra said, "but it doesn't happen very often, and my skin's getting tougher every year."

"I wish I had skin like that," Sam said enviously. Then he turned to me. "How come you wear the same suit all the time?" he asked.

I glanced down at the suit I'd been buried alive in. I'd meant to ask for some new clothes but had forgotten.

"I like it," I said.

"I've never seen a kid wearing a suit like that before," Sam said.

"Not unless at a wedding or a funeral. Are you forced to wear it?"

"No," I said.

"Did you ask your parents if you could join the Cirque?" Evra said then, to distract Sam's attention.

"No," Sam sighed. "I told them about it, of course, but I figured it would be best to take it in stages. I won't tell them until just before I leave, or maybe not until I'm gone."

"You still plan to join?" I asked.

"You bet!" Sam said. "I know you tried putting me off, but I'll get in somehow. You wait. I'll keep coming around, I'll read books and learn everything there is to know about freak shows, then I'll go to your boss and state my case. He won't be able to turn me down."

Evra and I smiled at each other. We knew Sam's dream would never lead to anything, but hadn't the heart to tell him.

We went to see an old deserted railway station later on, about two kilometres away, which Sam had told us about.

"It's great," he said. "They used to work on trains there, repair and paint them and stuff like that. It was a busy station in its day. Then a new firm set up closer to the city and this place went bust. It's a great place to play. There are rusty old railway tracks, empty sheds, a guard house, and a couple of ancient train carriages."

"Is it safe?" Evra asked.

"My mum says it isn't," Sam told us. "It's one of the few places she tells me to stay away from. She says I could fall through the roof of one of the carriages or trip on a rail or something. But I've been there loads of times and nothing's happened."

It was another sunny day and we were strolling along slowly under the cover of the trees, when I smelled something strange. I stopped and sniffed the air. Evra could smell it too.

"What is that?" I asked.

"I don't know," he said, sniffing the air beside me. "Which way is it coming from?"

"I can't tell," I said. It was a thick, heavy, sour smell.

Sam hadn't smelled anything and was walking on ahead of us. He realized we weren't beside him, stopped and turned to see what was keeping us.

"What's wrong?" he asked. "Why aren't you—"

"*Gotcha!*" a voice yelled behind me, and before I could move I felt a firm hand grab my shoulder and spin me around. I glimpsed a large, hairy face, and then I was falling backwards, thrown off-balance by the force of the hand.

CHAPTER SIXTEEN

I LANDED awkwardly and sprained my arm. I gave a shout of pain, then tried twisting away from the hairy figure above me. Before I could, he was crouching by my side, a fierce look on his face.

"Oh, hey, man, I didn't hurt you, did I?" He had a jolly voice and I realized my life wasn't in danger; the look on his face was one of concern, not anger.

"I didn't mean to spook you so much," the man said. "I was just trying to scare you a little, man, for fun."

I sat up and rubbed my elbow. "I'm OK," I said.

"You're sure? It ain't broken, is it? I've got herbs that can help, if it is."

"Herbs can't mend broken bones," Sam said. He'd tracked back and was standing beside Evra.

"They sure can't," the stranger agreed, "but they can elevate you to plains of consciousness where worldly concerns like broken bones are nothing but minor blips on the cosmic map." He paused and stroked his beard. "Of course, they burn out your brain cells too ..."

Sam's blank face showed that even *he* hadn't understood that long sentence.

"I'm OK," I said again. I stood and rotated the arm. "I just twisted it. It'll be fine in a couple of minutes."

"Man, that's good to hear," the stranger sighed. "I'd hate to be the cause of bodily harm. Hurt's a bad trip, man."

I studied him in more detail. He was big, chubby, with a bushy black beard and long scraggly hair. His clothes were dirty and he couldn't have had a bath recently, because he stank to high heaven. That's what the strange smell had been. He was so friendly-looking, it made me feel foolish thinking about how I'd been afraid of him.

"Are you kids locals?" the man asked.

"I am," Sam said. "These two are with the circus."

"Circus?" The man smiled. "There's a circus around here? Oh, man, how did I miss it? Where is it? I love the circus. I never pass up a chance to see clowns in action."

"It's not that sort of circus," Sam told him. "It's a freak-show."

"A freak-show?" The man stared at Sam, then at Evra, whose scales and colour clearly marked him out as one of the performers. "Are you part of a freak-show, man?" he asked.

Evra nodded shyly.

"They don't maltreat you, do they?" the man asked. "They don't whip you or under-feed you or make you do things you don't want?"

"No," Evra smiled.

"You're there of your own free will?"

"Yes," Evra said. "All of us are. It's our home."

"Oh. Well, that's OK," the man said, smiling once more. "You hear rumours about these small travelling shows. You ..." He slapped his forehead. "Oh man, I haven't introduced myself, have I? I'm so dumb sometimes. R.V.'s the name."

"R.V.? That's a funny name," I remarked.

He coughed with embarrassment. "Well," he said, lowering his voice to a whisper, "it's short for Reggie Veggie."

"*Reggie Veggie?*" I laughed.

"Yeah," he grimaced. "Reggie's my real name. Reggie Veggie's what they called me in school, because I'm a vegetarian. Well, I never liked that, so I asked them to call me R.V. instead. Some did, but not many." He looked miserable at the memory. "You can call me Reggie Veggie if you want," he told us.

"R.V. is fine by me," I assured him.

"Me too," Evra said.

"And me," Sam added.

"Cool!" R.V. brightened up. "So, that's my name out in the open. How about you three?"

"Darren Shan," I told him, and we shook hands.

"Sam Grest."

"Evra Von."

"Evra Von what?" R.V. asked, as I had when I first met Evra.

"Just plain Von," Evra said.

"Oh." R.V. smiled. "Cool!"

R.V. was an eco warrior, here to stop a road being built. He was a member of NOP – Nature's Opposing Protectors – and had travelled the length and breadth of the country, saving forests and lakes and animals and famous landmarks.

He offered to show us round his camp and we jumped at the chance. The railway station could wait. This was an opportunity that wouldn't arise every day.

He talked about the environment non-stop as we walked. He told us about all the lousy things being done to Mother Nature, the forests we were destroying, the rivers we were polluting, the air we were poisoning, the animals we were driving to extinction.

"And this is all in our own country!" he said. "I'm not talking

86

about stuff happening somewhere else. This is what we're doing to our own land!"

NOP were fighting to save the earth from greedy, dangerous humans who didn't care what they did to it. They journeyed up and down the country, trying to make other people aware of the dangers. They gave out pamphlets and books about how to protect the environment.

"But raising awareness ain't enough," R.V. told us. "It's a start, but we must do more. We have to stop the pollution and destruction of the countryside. Take this place: they were going to build a road through an old burial mound, a place where druids buried their dead, thousands of years ago. Can you imagine that, man? Destroying a part of history, just to save drivers ten or twenty minutes!"

R.V. shook his head sadly. "These are crazy times, man," he said. "The things we're doing to this planet ... In the future – assuming there is one – people will look back on what we've done and call us idiotic barbarians."

He was very passionate about the environment and, after listening to him for a while, so were Sam, Evra and me. I hadn't thought about it much before, but after a couple of hours with R.V., I realized I should have. As R.V. said, those who don't think and act now can't complain when the world crumbles around their ears later.

His camp-site was an interesting place. The people – twenty or so – slept in hand-made huts which had been built out of branches and leaves and shrubs. Most were as dirty and smelly as R.V., but they were also cheerful and kind and generous.

"How did you stop the road from being built?" Sam asked.

"We dug tunnels beneath the land," R.V. said. "And we sabotaged the machines they sent in. And we alerted the media. Rich cats hate having cameras pointed at them. One TV news crew is as good as twenty active warriors."

Evra asked R.V. if they ever fought hand to hand. R.V. said NOP didn't believe in violent confrontation, but we could see from the look on his face that he wasn't happy about that. "If I had my way," he said quietly, "we'd give as good as we got. We're too nice sometimes. Man, if I was in charge, we'd give those turkeys a taste of what-for!"

R.V. invited us to stay for lunch. It wasn't very nice food — there was no meat, just loads of vegetables and rice and fruit — but we ate plenty, to be polite.

They had lots of mushrooms as well — large and oddly coloured — but R.V. wouldn't let us eat any of those.

"When you're older, man," he chuckled.

We left shortly after lunch. The members of NOP had duties and jobs to be getting on with and we didn't want to be in the way.

R.V. told us we could come back any time, but that they'd probably be moving on in a couple of days.

"We've almost won the fight here," he said. "Another few days and it'll be time to strike out for pastures new. Battles come and go, man, but the war is never ending."

We waved goodbye and hit for home.

"That R.V.'s strange," Sam said after a while. "Imagine giving up everything to go off and fight for animals and the countryside."

"He's doing what he believes in," Evra said.

"I know," Sam said. "And I'm glad he's doing it. We need people like him. It's a pity there aren't more of his kind. Still, it's an odd way to live, isn't it? You'd have to be very dedicated. I don't think I could become an environmental warrior."

"Me neither," I agreed.

"I could," Evra said.

"You could not," I snorted.

"Why not?" he pouted. "I could take my snake and live with them and fight with them."

"You couldn't," I insisted.

"Why not?" he asked.

"Because you're not smelly enough!" I laughed.

Evra pulled a face, then grinned. "They *were* a bit on the pongy side, weren't they?" he admitted.

"They smell worse than my feet when I haven't changed my socks for a week!" Sam guffawed.

"Still," Evra said, "I can think of lots of worse ways to spend my time when I grow up. I'd like to be like R.V. when I'm older."

"Me too," Sam said.

I shrugged. "I guess I could get used to it," I agreed.

We were in high spirits and talked about NOP and R.V. the whole way back to camp. None of us had any idea of the trouble the nice eco warrior would soon create ... or the tragedy he would unwittingly cause.

CHAPTER SEVENTEEN

WE PASSED the next few days in leisurely fashion. Evra and me were kept busy with our chores and with feeding the Little People. I'd tried talking to a couple of the silent blue-hooded creatures, but not one of them so much as looked at me when I spoke.

It was impossible to tell them apart. One stood out because he – or she (or it) – was taller than the others, and one was shorter, and another limped on his left leg. But the rest looked exactly alike.

Sam was helping out more and more around the camp. We didn't take him with us when we went hunting, but let him lend a hand with most of our other jobs. He was a hard worker, determined to impress us and earn himself a full-time position with the Cirque.

I didn't see much of Mr Crepsley. He knew I had to be up early to hunt for the Little People's food, so he left me alone most of the time. I was happy that way; I didn't want him bugging me about drinking human blood.

Then Cormac Limbs arrived, early one morning, which caused great excitement.

"You've got to see this guy," Evra said, dragging me behind him. "He's the most amazing performer who ever lived."

There was already a large crowd around Cormac when we arrived at Mr Tall's van (where he had reported to). People were slapping him on the back and asking what he'd been up to and where he'd been. He smiled at everybody, shook hands and answered their questions. He might have been a star but he wasn't big-headed.

"Evra Von!" he shouted when he saw the snake-boy. He reached over and gave Evra a hug. "How's my favourite two-legged reptile?"

"Fine," Evra said.

"Did you shed your skin lately?" Cormac asked.

"Not recently," Evra said.

"Remember," Cormac said, "I want it when you do. It's valuable. Human snake-skin is worth more than gold in some countries."

"You can have as much of it as you like," Evra assured him. Then he pushed me forward. "Cormac, this is Darren Shan, a friend of mine. He's new at the Cirque and has never seen you before."

"Never seen Cormac Limbs?!?" Cormac shouted, pretending to be upset. "How can this be? I thought everybody in the world had seen the magnificent Cormac Limbs in action."

"I've never even heard of you," I told him.

He clutched his chest as though suffering a heart-attack.

"What is it you do?" I asked.

Cormac looked around at the crowd. "Shall I give a demonstration?"

"Oh yes!" they shouted eagerly.

Cormac looked at Mr Tall, standing at the back of the crowd. Mr Tall sighed and nodded. "You may as well," he said. "They won't leave you alone until you do."

"Very well," Cormac said. "Stand back and give me room."

The crowd moved back immediately. I started to move with them, but Cormac laid a hand on my shoulder and told me to stay.

"Now," he said to the crowd, "I've been travelling for ages and I'm too tired to go through my entire routine, so we'll keep this short and sweet."

He made his right hand into a fist, then stuck out his index finger. "Darren, will you place this finger in your mouth?" he asked.

I glanced at Evra, who signalled for me to do as Cormac asked.

"Now," Cormac said, "bite down on it, please."

I bit softly.

"Harder," Cormac said.

I bit slightly harder.

"Come on, boy," Cormac shouted. "Put some backbone in it. Work those jaws. Are you a shark or a mouse?"

OK. He wanted me to bite hard? Then I would.

I opened my mouth and bit down quickly, meaning to give him a shock. Instead, I was the one who was shocked, because I bit *clean through the finger and snapped it right off!*

I fell back in terror and spat the dead finger from my mouth. My eyes shot up at Cormac Limbs. I expected him to scream, but he only laughed and held up his hand.

There was no blood where I'd bitten the finger off, only a white, jagged stump. As I watched, the most amazing thing happened, *the finger began to grow back!*

I thought I must be imagining it, but as the seconds passed, it continued to grow and soon it was full length again. Cormac held it rigidly in place a few seconds longer, then flexed it in and out to show it was as good as new.

The crowd cheered and I felt my heart settle in my chest.

I looked down at the ground, where I'd spat out the finger, and saw it beginning to rot. Within a minute it was nothing more than a greyish mound of mould.

"Sorry if I frightened you," Cormac said, giving my head a pat.

"That's OK," I told him. "I should have learned by now to expect the unexpected round here. Can I feel the new finger?" He nodded. It felt no different to any of the others. "How do you do it?" I asked, amazed. "Is it an illusion?"

"No illusion," he said. "It's why they call me Cormac *Limbs*. I've been able to grow new limbs – fingers, toes, arms, legs – ever since I was a nipper. My parents discovered my talent when I had an accident with a kitchen knife and cut off part of my nose. I can grow virtually any part of my body anew. Except my head. I haven't tried cutting that off. Best not to tempt fate."

"Doesn't it hurt?" I asked.

"A little," he said, "but not much. When one of my limbs gets cut off, a new one starts to grow almost immediately, so there's only a second or two of pain. It's a bit like—"

"Come, come!" Mr Tall bellowed, cutting him short. "We don't have time for a detailed description. This show has been idle far too long. It's time we entertained the public again, before they forget about us or think we've retired.

"People," he shouted to the crowd and clapped his hands together. "Spread the word. The lull is over. The show goes on tonight!"

CHAPTER EIGHTEEN

THE CAMP was buzzing with activity all afternoon. People were rushing about like ants. A large number were working on putting together the circus tent. I hadn't seen it before. It was an impressive sight when finished, tall and round and red, decorated with pictures of the performers.

Evra and me were kept busy, hammering pegs into the ground to hold the tent in place, arranging seats inside, setting up the stage for the show, preparing props for the performers (we had to find tin cans and nuts and bolts for Rhamus Twobellies to eat, help move the Wolf Man's cage inside the tent, and so on).

It was a huge operation but it moved with incredible speed. Everyone in the camp knew their place and what was expected of them, and there was never any real panic over the course of the day. Everybody worked as part of a team and things came together smoothly.

Sam turned up early in the afternoon. I would have kept him around to help with the work, but Evra said he'd be in the way, so we sent him packing. He was upset and slouched off in a sulk, kicking an empty tin can along in front of him. I felt sorry for him, then realized how I could cheer him up.

"Sam! Wait a minute!" I shouted. "I'll be back in a tick," I told Evra, then rushed off to Mr Tall's van.

I knocked once on the door and it opened instantly. Mr Tall was standing inside and, before I could say a word, he held out two tickets for entry to the Cirque Du Freak.

I stared at the tickets, then at Mr Tall. "How did you know ...?"

"I have my ways," he replied with a smile.

"I haven't any money," I warned him.

"I'll take it out of your wages," he said.

I frowned. "You don't pay me anything."

His smile widened. "Clever old me." He handed over the tickets and closed the door in my face before I could thank him.

I hurried back to Sam and passed on the tickets.

"What are these?" he asked.

"Tickets for tonight's show," I told him. "One for you and one for R.V."

"Oh, wow!" Sam quickly stuck the tickets into his pocket, as if he was afraid they might blow away or vanish. "Thanks, Darren."

"No problem," I said. "The only thing is, it's a late show. We're starting at eleven and it won't be over till nearly one in the morning. Will you be able to make it?"

"Sure," Sam said. "I'll sneak out. Mum and Dad go to bed at half past nine every night. They're early birds."

"If you get caught," I warned him, "don't tell them where you're going."

"My lips are sealed," he promised, then set off at a run to find R.V.

Except for a quick dinner, there was no further break between then and the start of the show. While Evra left to groom his snake, I set up candles inside the circus tent. There were also five huge chandeliers to be hung, four above the crowd, one over the stage, but the Little People handled those.

Mags — a pretty woman who sold toys and sweets during the breaks — asked me to help her get the trays ready, so I spent an hour stacking candy webs and edible "glass" statues and strands of the Wolf Man's hair. There was a new novelty I hadn't seen before: a small model of Cormac Limbs. When you cut a part of it off, a new piece grew in its place. I asked Mags how it worked but she didn't know.

"It's one of Mr Tall's inventions," she said. "He makes a lot of this stuff himself."

I chopped the head off the model and tried peering down the neck, to see what was inside, but a new head grew before I could.

"The models don't last for ever," Mags said. "They rot after a few months."

"Do you tell people that when they're buying them?" I asked.

"Of course," she said. "Mr Tall insists we let the customers know exactly what they're buying. He doesn't approve of conning people."

Mr Crepsley sent for me half an hour before the show began. He was dressing in his stage costume when I entered.

"Polish Madam Octa's cage," he ordered, "then brush your suit down and clean yourself up."

"Why?" I asked.

"You are going on with me," he said.

My eyes lit up. "You mean I'm part of the act?" I gasped.

"A small part," he said. "You can bring the cage on and play the flute when it is Madam Octa's time to spin a web over my mouth."

"Mr Tall normally does that, doesn't he?"

"Normally," Mr Crepsley agreed, "but we are short on performers tonight, so he is going to be performing himself. Besides, you are better suited to assisting than him."

"How so?" I asked.

"You look creepier," he said. "With your pale face and that awful suit, you look like something out of a horror film."

That gave me a bit of a shock. I'd never thought I was creepy looking! I glanced in a mirror and realized I did look a bit of a fright. Because I hadn't drunk human blood, I was much paler than I should have been. The dirty suit made me look even more ghost-like. I made up my mind to find something new to wear in the morning.

The show started promptly at eleven. I hadn't expected much of a crowd — we were in the middle of nowhere and hadn't had much time to notify people about the show — but the tent was packed.

"Where did they all come from?" I whispered to Evra as we watched Mr Tall introduce the Wolf Man.

"Everywhere," he replied quietly. "People always know when one of our shows is on. Besides, though he only told us about it today, Mr Tall probably knew we'd be playing tonight ever since we set up camp."

I watched the show from the wings, enjoying it even more than the first time I'd seen it, because now I knew the people involved and felt like part of the family.

Hans Hands went on after the Wolf Man, followed by Rhamus Twobellies. We had our first break, then Mr Tall took to the stage and darted round the place, never seeming to move, merely vanishing from one spot and appearing somewhere new. Next up was Truska, then it was my turn to go on stage with Mr Crepsley and Madam Octa.

The lights were low but my vampire vision helped me pick out the faces of Sam and R.V. in the crowd. They were stunned to see me, but clapped louder than anybody else. I had to hide my smile of delight: Mr Crepsley had told me to look miserable and glum, to impress the crowd.

I stood to one side as Mr Crepsley made a speech about how deadly Madam Octa was, then opened the door to her cage as an assistant led a goat on to the stage.

There was a loud, angry gasp when Madam Octa killed the goat ... it came from R.V. I knew then that I shouldn't have invited him – I'd forgotten how fond of animals he was – but it was too late to withdraw my invitation.

I was slightly nervous when it was my turn to play the flute and control Madam Octa, feeling every set of eyes in the tent focus on me. I'd never performed to a crowd before and for a few seconds I was afraid my lips wouldn't work or I'd forget the tune. But once I started blowing and sending my thoughts to Madam Octa, I settled into my stride.

As she weaved her web across Mr Crepsley's lips, it struck me that I could get rid of him now if I wanted.

I could make her bite him.

The idea shocked me. I'd thought about killing him before, but never seriously, and not since we'd joined the Cirque. Now here he was, his life in my hands. All it would take was one "slip". I could claim it was an accident. Nobody would be able to prove otherwise.

I watched the spider move back and forth, up and down, her poisonous fangs glinting under the lights of the chandelier. The heat from the candles seemed immense. I was sweating freely. It occurred to me that I could blame the slip of my fingers on the sweat.

Over his mouth she spun her web. His hands were down by his sides. He wouldn't be able to stop her. One wrong toot on the flute was all it needed. One broken note to sever the train of thought between the two of us, and ...

I didn't do it. I played perfectly and safely. I wasn't sure why I'd spared the vampire. Maybe because Mr Tall might know I'd killed him. Maybe because I needed Mr Crepsley to teach me how to survive. Maybe because I didn't want to become a killer.

Or maybe, just maybe, because I was starting to like the vampire. After all, he'd brought me to the Cirque and made me part of his act. I wouldn't have met Evra and Sam if it hadn't been for him. He'd been kind to me, as kind as he could be.

Whatever the reason, I didn't let Madam Octa kill her master, and at the end of the act we took our bows and exited together.

"You thought about killing me," Mr Crepsley said softly once we were backstage.

"What do you mean?" I played dumb.

"You know what I mean," he said. There was a pause. "It would not have worked. I milked most of the poison from her fangs before we went on. Killing the goat took the rest out of her."

"It was a test?" I stared at him, and my hatred grew again. "I thought you were being nice to me!" I cried. "And all the time it was just a rotten old test!"

His face was grave. "I had to know," he said. "I had to know if I could rely on you."

"Well, listen to this," I growled, standing on my toes in order to go eyeball to eyeball with him. "Your test was useless. I didn't kill you this time, but if I ever get the chance again, I'll take it!"

I stormed off in a huff without another word, too upset to stick around to see Cormac Limbs or the end of the show, feeling betrayed, even though deep down I knew what he said made sense.

CHAPTER NINETEEN

I WAS still upset the next morning. Evra kept asking me what was wrong but I wouldn't tell him. I didn't want him to know I'd been thinking of killing Mr Crepsley.

Evra told me he'd met Sam and R.V. after the show. "Sam loved it," Evra said, "especially Cormac Limbs. You should have stayed to see Cormac in action. When he sawed his legs off ..."

"I'll see him next time," I said. "How did R.V. take it?"

Evra frowned. "He wasn't happy."

"Upset about the goat?" I asked.

"Yes," Evra said, "but not just that. I said we bought the goat from a butcher, so it would have been killed anyway. It was the Wolf Man, the snake and Mr Crepsley's spider which bothered him the most."

"What was wrong with *them*?" I asked.

"He was afraid they weren't being treated right. He didn't like the idea of them being locked in cages. I told him they weren't, except for the spider. I said the Wolf Man was quiet as a lamb off-stage. And I showed him my snake and how she slept with me."

"Did he believe you about the Wolf Man?" I asked.

"I think so," Evra said, "though he still seemed suspicious

when leaving. And he was *very* interested in their eating habits. He wanted to know what we fed them, how often, and where we got the food. We'll have to be careful with R.V. He could cause problems. Luckily, he should be leaving in a day or two, but until then: caution!"

We passed the day quietly. Sam didn't turn up until late in the afternoon and none of us was in much of a mood for playing. It was a cloudy day and we were all a bit out of sorts. Sam only stayed for half an hour, then trotted off home again.

Mr Crepsley summoned me to his tent shortly after sunset. I wasn't going to go, but decided it was best not to annoy him too much. He was my guardian, after all, and could probably have me booted out of the Cirque Du Freak.

"What do you want?" I snapped when I arrived.

"Stand over here, where I can see you better," the vampire said.

He tilted my head backwards with his bony fingers and rolled up my eyelids to check the whites of my eyes. He told me to open my mouth and peered down my throat. Then he checked my pulse and reflexes.

"How do you feel?" he asked.

"Tired," I said.

"Weak?" he asked. "Sick?"

"A bit."

He grunted. "Have you been drinking much blood lately?" he asked.

"As much as I'm meant to," I said.

"But no human blood?"

"No," I said softly.

"OK," he said. "Get ready. We are going out."

"Hunting?" I asked.

He shook his head. "To see a friend."

I got up on his back outside the tent and he began running.

When we were clear of the camp he flitted and the world blurred around us.

I didn't take much notice of where we were going. I was more concerned with my suit. I'd forgotten to get new clothes, and now, the more I examined it, the worse it seemed.

There were dozens of small holes and rips, and the colour was a shade greyer than it was supposed to be, because of the dirt and dust. Many strands of thread and fibres had come loose, and every time I shook an arm or a leg, I appeared to be shedding hairs.

I'd never been very worried about clothes, but I didn't want to look like a *tramp*. Tomorrow I would definitely find something new to wear.

After a while we reached a city and Mr Crepsley slowed. He stopped outside the back of a tall building. I wanted to ask where we were, but he put a finger to his lips and made the sign for silence.

The back door was locked but Mr Crepsley laid a hand over it and clicked the fingers of his other hand. It opened instantly. He led the way through a long, dark corridor, then up a set of stairs and on to a brightly-lit hallway.

After a few minutes, we came to a white desk. Mr Crepsley glanced around to make sure we were alone, then rang the bell that hung from one of the walls.

A figure appeared behind the glass wall on the other side of the desk. The door in the glass wall opened and a ginger-haired man in a white uniform and green mask stepped through. He looked like a doctor.

"How may I—" he began, then stopped. "Larten Crepsley! What the hell are you doing here, you old devil?"

The man pulled down his mask and I saw he was grinning.

"Hello, Jimmy," Mr Crepsley said. The two shook hands and smiled at each other. "Long time no see."

"Not as long as I thought it would be," the man called Jimmy said. "I heard you'd been killed. An old foe had finally rammed a stake through your rotten heart, or so the story went."

"You should not believe everything you hear," Mr Crepsley said. He placed a hand on my shoulder and nudged me forward. "Jimmy, this is Darren Shan, a travelling companion of mine. Darren, this is Jimmy Ovo, an old friend and the world's finest pathologist."

"Hello," I said.

"Pleased to meet you," Jimmy said, shaking my hand. "You aren't a ... I mean, do you belong to *the club*?"

"He is a vampire," Mr Crepsley said.

"Only half of me," I snapped. "I'm not a full vampire."

"Please," Jimmy winced. "Don't use that word. I know what you guys are, and I'm fine about it, but that 'V' word never fails to freak me out." He shivered playfully. "I think it's because of all the horror movies I watched when I was a kid. I know you're not like those cinema monsters, but it's hard to get the image out of my mind."

"What's a pathologist do?" I asked.

"I cut corpses open to see how they died," Jimmy explained. "I don't do it with many bodies — just those who died in suspicious circumstances."

"This is a city morgue," Mr Crepsley said. "They store bodies that arrive dead at the hospital, or die whilst there."

"Is that where you keep them?" I asked Jimmy, pointing at the room behind the glass wall.

"Yup," he said cheerfully. He swung up a section of the desk and invited us through.

I was nervous. I expected to see dozens of tables, heaped high with sliced-open bodies. But it wasn't like that. There was one dead body, covered from head to toe with a long sheet, but that was the only one I could spot. Otherwise it was a huge, well-lit room, with large filing cabinets set in the walls and lots of medical equipment scattered around the place.

"How is business?" Mr Crepsley asked as we sat on three chairs near the corpse on the table. Jimmy and Mr Crepsley took no notice of the dead person and, as I didn't want to look out of place, neither did I.

"Slow enough," Jimmy answered. "The weather's been good and there haven't been many road accidents. No strange diseases, no food epidemics, no collapsing buildings. By the way," he added, "I had an old friend of yours in here a few years back."

"Oh?" Mr Crepsley responded politely. "Who was that?"

Jimmy sniffed heavily through his nose, then cleared his throat.

"*Gavner Purl?*" Mr Crepsley hooted with delight. "How is the old dog — as clumsy as ever?"

They started talking about their friend, Gavner Purl. I glanced around curiously while they were speaking, wondering where the bodies were kept. Finally, when they paused for breath, I asked Jimmy. He got to his feet and told me to follow. He led the way to the large filing cabinets and pulled one of the drawers out.

There was a hissing sound and a cloud of cold air rose from inside the drawer. When it cleared, I saw a sheet-covered form and realized the filing cabinets weren't filing cabinets at all. They were refrigerated coffins!

"We store the bodies here until we're ready," Jimmy said, "or until their next of kin come to collect them."

I looked around the room, quickly counting the many rows of drawer doors. "Is there a body behind all of these?" I asked.

Jimmy shook his head. "We've only got six guests at the moment, not counting the one on the table. Like I said, it's quiet. Mind you, even during our busiest times, most of our storage space goes unused. It's rare for us to be half full. We just like to be prepared for the worst."

"Any fresh bodies in stock?" Mr Crepsley asked.

"Wait a minute and I'll check," Jimmy said. He consulted a large pad and flicked through a few pages. "There's a man in his thirties," Jimmy said. "Died in a car crash just over eight hours ago."

"Nothing fresher?" Mr Crepsley asked.

"Afraid not," Jimmy replied.

Mr Crepsley sighed. "It will have to do."

"Wait a minute," I said. "You're not going to drink from a dead person, are you?"

"No," Mr Crepsley said. He reached inside his cloak and produced several of the small bottles in which he stored his supply of human blood. "I have come for a refill."

"You can't!" I gasped.

"Why not?" he asked.

"It isn't right. It's not fair to drink from the dead. Besides, the blood will have turned sour."

"It will not be at its best," Mr Crepsley agreed, "but it will do for bottling. And I disagree: a corpse is the ideal person to drain, since it has no use for the blood. It will take a lot to fill these bottles. Too much to take from a living person."

"Not if you took a bit from several," I protested.

"True," he said. "But that would require time, effort and risk. It is easier this way."

"Darren doesn't speak like a vampire," Jimmy remarked.

"He is still learning," Mr Crepsley grunted. "Now, lead the way to the body, please. We have not got all night."

I knew it would be pointless to argue further, so I shut my mouth and followed silently behind them.

Jimmy slid out the body of a tall, blonde-haired man and whipped back the sheet. There was a nasty bruise on the dead man's head and his body was very white, but otherwise he looked like he might be sleeping.

Mr Crepsley made a long, deep cut across the man's chest, baring his heart. He arranged the bottles beside the corpse, then got out a tube and stuck one end into the first of the bottles. He stuck the other end into the dead man's heart, then wrapped his fist around the organ and squeezed it like a pump.

Slowly, blood crept along the tube and into the bottle. When it was nearly full, Mr Crepsley pulled the tube out and jammed a cork into the neck of the bottle. He stuck the mouth of the tube into the second bottle and started filling that one.

Raising the first bottle, he swallowed a mouthful and rolled it around his gums, as though tasting wine. "Good," he grunted, licking his lips. "It is pure. We can use it."

He filled eight bottles, then turned to me with a serious look on his face.

"Darren," he said, "I know you are reluctant to drink human blood, but it is time you got over your fear."

"No," I said immediately.

"Come now, Darren," he growled. "This person is dead. His blood is no good to him any more."

"I can't," I said. "Not from a corpse."

"But you will not drink from a live person!" Mr Crepsley exploded. "You will have to drink human blood eventually. This is the best way to start."

"Um, listen, guys," Jimmy said. "If you're going to feed, I think I should get out of—"

"Quiet!" Mr Crepsley snapped. His eyes were burning into me. "You have to drink," he said firmly. "You are a vampire's assistant. It is time you behaved like one."

"Not tonight," I begged. "Another time. When we go hunting. From a living person. I can't drink from a corpse. It's disgusting."

Mr Crepsley sighed and shook his head. "One night you will realize how silly you are being," he said. "I just hope, by that time, you are not beyond being saved."

Mr Crepsley thanked Jimmy Ovo for his help and the two got to talking about the past and their friends. I sat by myself while they chatted, feeling miserable, wondering how long I could go without human blood.

When they were finished, we walked downstairs. Jimmy came with us and waved goodbye. He was a nice man and I was sorry we'd had to meet under such dark circumstances.

Mr Crepsley didn't say anything the whole way home and, when we arrived back at the Cirque Du Freak, he angrily tossed me to one side and pointed a finger at me.

"If you die," he said, "it is not my fault."

"OK," I replied.

"Stupid boy," he grumbled, then stormed off to his coffin.

I stayed up a while longer and watched the sun rising. I thought a lot about my situation and what would happen when my strength faded and I began to die. A half-vampire who wouldn't drink blood; it would have been funny if it wasn't so deadly.

What should I do? That was the question which kept me awake long after the sun had risen. What should I do? Abandon my principles and drink human blood? Or stay true to my humanity and ... *die*?

CHAPTER TWENTY

I STAYED inside my tent most of the day and didn't even go out to say hello to Sam when he came round. My spirits were at their lowest ever. I didn't feel like I belonged anywhere any longer. I couldn't be a human and wouldn't be a vampire. I was torn between the two.

I got a lot of sleep that night and the next day felt better. The sun was shining and, although I knew my problems hadn't gone away, I was able to overlook them for the time being.

Evra's snake was poorly. She'd picked up a virus and Evra had to stay in to look after her.

When Sam turned up, we decided to visit that old deserted railway station of his. Evra didn't mind being left behind. He'd come with us another time.

The railway station was cool. There was a huge circular yard, paved with cracked stones; a three-storey house which had served as the guard's house, a couple of old sheds, and several abandoned train carriages. There were also railway tracks running everywhere you looked, overgrown with weeds and grass.

Sam and I walked along some of the tracks and pretended we were on tightropes high above the ground. Every time one of us slipped, he had to scream and pretend to fall heavily to earth. I was much better at the game than Sam, because my vampire powers meant my sense of balance was better than any human's.

We explored a few of the old carriages. A couple were in a sorry state, but most were OK. Very dusty and dirty, but otherwise in good condition. I couldn't understand why they'd been left here to rot.

We climbed on top of the roof of one of the carriages and stretched out to enjoy the sun.

"You know what we should do?" Sam said after a while.

"What?" I asked.

"Become blood-brothers."

I propped myself up on an elbow and stared. "Blood-brothers?" I asked. "What for? And how's it done?"

"It'd be fun," he said. "We each make a small cut in one of our hands, then join them together and swear an oath to be best friends for ever."

"That sounds all right," I agreed. "Do you have a knife?"

"We can use some glass," Sam said. He slid over to the edge of the roof, reached down and snapped a piece of glass out of one of the carriage windows. When he returned, he made a small cut in the fleshy part of his palm, then handed me the glass.

I was about to cut my palm when I remembered the vampire blood in my veins. I didn't think a small amount could do Sam any harm, but then again ...

I lowered the glass and shook my head.

"No," I said. "I don't want to do it."

"Come on," Sam urged. "There's no need to be afraid. You only have to make a small cut."

"No," I said again.

"Coward!" he snorted. "You're afraid! Chicken! Coward!" He

began to sing: "Cowardly, cowardly custard, buy yourself some mustard."

"OK, I'm a coward," I laughed. It was easier to lie than tell the truth. "Everybody's afraid of something. I didn't see you rushing to wash the Wolf Man the other day."

Sam pulled a face. "That's different."

"Horses for courses," I said smugly.

"What does that mean?" he asked.

"I'm not sure," I admitted. "It's something my dad used to say."

We joked about some more, then hopped down and crossed the yard to the guard's house. The doors had rotted off years ago and most of the glass in the windows had fallen out. We walked through a couple of small rooms, into a larger one, which had been the living room.

There was a huge hole in the middle of the floor, which we carefully avoided.

"Look up," Sam told me.

I did and discovered I was gazing directly at the roof. The floors between had fallen in some time over the years, and all that was left of them were jagged edges around the sides. I could see sunlight shining through several holes in the roof.

"Follow me," Sam said and led me to a staircase at the side of the room. He started up. I followed slowly, not sure if this was wise — the steps were creaky and looked as if they might collapse — but not wishing to be called a chicken twice in the same day.

We stopped at the third floor, where the stairs ran out. You could touch the roof from here, and we did.

"Can we get out on the roof?" I asked.

"Yes," Sam said, "but it's too dangerous. The slates are loose. You could slide off. Anyway, there's something better up here than the roof."

He set off along the side of the uppermost room of the house. The ledge was about half a metre wide most of the way, but I kept my back to the wall, not wanting to take any chances.

"This bit of floor won't collapse, will it?" I asked nervously.

"It never has before," Sam replied. "But there's a first time for everything."

"Thanks for setting my mind at ease," I grumbled.

Sam stopped a bit further on. I craned my neck so I could see past him, and realized we had come to a set of rafters. There were six or seven of them, long pieces of wood stretching from one side of the room to the other.

"This used to be the attic," Sam explained.

"I guessed that," I told him.

He looked back at me and grinned. "But can you guess what we're going to do next?" he asked.

I stared at him, then down at the rafters. "You can't mean ... You aren't going to ... You're going to walk across, right?"

"Right," he said, and set his left foot on the rafter.

"Sam, this isn't a good idea," I said. "You looked unsteady on the railway tracks. If you stumble up here ..."

"I won't," he said. "I was only fooling down below."

He set his other foot on the wooden rafter and began walking. He went slowly, his arms stretched out on either side. My heart was in my mouth. I was certain he'd fall. I glanced down and knew he wouldn't survive if he fell. There were four storeys if you included the basement. It was a long drop. A deadly one.

But Sam made it across safely to the other side, where he turned and took a bow.

"You're crazy!" I yelled.

"No," he said, "just brave. How about *you*? Care to chance it? It'd be easier for you than it was for me."

"What do you mean?" I asked.

"Chickens have wings!" he shouted.

That did it! I'd show him!

Taking a deep breath, I set across, moving quicker than Sam had, making full use of my vampire abilities. I didn't look down and tried not to think about what I was doing, and in a couple of seconds I was across and standing beside Sam.

"Wow!" He was impressed. "I didn't think you'd do it. Certainly not so quickly?"

"You don't travel with the Cirque without picking up a few tricks," I said, pleased with myself.

"Do you think *I* could go that fast?" Sam asked.

"I wouldn't try it," I advised him.

"I bet you can't do it again," he dared me.

"Just watch," I said, and darted back across, even faster.

We spent a fun few minutes crossing over and back, taking each of the rafters in turn. Then we crossed at the same time, on different rafters, yelling and laughing at one another.

Sam stopped in the middle of his rafter and turned to face me.

"Hey!" he shouted. "Let's play mirrors."

"What's that?" I asked.

"I do something and you have to copy me." He shook his left hand above his head. "Like this."

"Oh," I said, and shook my hand. "OK. As long as you don't jump to your death. That's the one thing I *won't* copy."

He laughed, then pulled a face. I pulled one too. Then he slowly stood on one leg. I did likewise. Next he bent and touched his toes. I followed his example. I couldn't wait until it was my turn. I'd do a few things – like jump from one rafter to the next – that he couldn't possibly copy. For once, I was glad of my vampire blood.

Naturally, that was the moment when it went and let me down.

There was no warning. One second I was beginning to stand, having bent to touch my toes. The next my head was spinning, my arms were flapping and my legs were shaking.

This wasn't my first dizzy spell — I'd had several recently — but I hadn't taken much notice before: just sat down and waited for the dizziness to pass. This time was different. I was four storeys up. There was nowhere to sit.

I tried lowering myself, thinking I could cling to the rafter and crawl to safety. But before I could get low enough, my feet slipped from beneath me ... and I fell!

CHAPTER TWENTY-ONE

ALTHOUGH MY vampire blood was responsible for getting me into the mess on the rafters, it also saved my life.

As I fell, I stuck out an arm — more in hope than anything else — and my hand caught the rafter. If I'd been an ordinary human boy I wouldn't have had the strength to hold on. But I wasn't ordinary. I was a half-vampire. And even though I was dizzy, I was able to grab tight and cling on.

I swung above the four-storey drop, eyes shut, hanging on by those four slim fingers and my thumb.

"Darren! Hang on!" Sam shouted. He didn't need to tell me that — I was hardly going to let go!

"I'm coming over," Sam said. "I'll be there as fast as I can. Don't let go. And don't panic."

He went on talking as he made his way across, calming me down, telling me it would be all right, he'd rescue me, I had to relax, everything was fine.

His words helped. They gave me something apart from the drop to think about. If not for Sam, I'd have been a goner.

I felt him start out along my rafter. The wood creaked, and for one terrible moment I thought the weight would cause it to break and send both of us plummeting to our deaths. But it held and he closed the gap, crawling along on his stomach, quickly but carefully.

Sam paused when he reached me.

"Now," he said, "I'm going to grab your wrist with my right hand. I'll do it slowly. Don't move while I'm doing it, and don't snatch at me with your free hand. OK?"

"OK," I said.

I felt his hand close over my wrist.

"Don't let go of the rafter," he said.

"I won't," I promised.

"I don't have the strength to pull you up," he told me, "so I'm going to swing you from one side to the other. Stretch your free arm out. When you're able, make a grab for the rafter. If you miss, don't panic, I'll still be holding on. If you get a grip, stay still for a few seconds and give your body a chance to relax. Then we can haul you up. Got that?"

"Got it, captain," I said, grinning nervously.

"OK. Here goes. And remember: everything will be all right. It's going to work. You will survive."

He began swinging me, lightly at first, then a bit harder. I was tempted to snatch at the rafter after a few swings but forced myself to wait. When I felt I was swinging high enough, I stretched out my fingers, concentrated on the thin plank of wood, and grabbed.

I caught it!

I was able to relax a little then and rest the muscles of my right arm.

"Do you feel ready to pull yourself up?" Sam asked.

"Yes," I said.

"I'll help you get your upper body up," he said. "When your belly is safe across the rafter, I'll get out of the way and give you room to draw your legs up."

Sam put his right hand on the collar of my shirt and jacket —
to catch me if I slipped — and helped yank me upwards.

I scraped my chest and belly on the rafter but the pain didn't
bother me. In fact, I welcomed it: it meant I was alive.

When I was safe, Sam backed off and I got my legs up. I
crawled after him, moving slower than necessary. When I reached
the ledge, I stayed crouched low and didn't stand until we got to
the stairs. Then I leant against the wall and let out a long,
shuddering sigh of relief.

"Wow," Sam said to the left of me. "That was *fun!* Do you
want to do it again?"

I *think* he was joking.

CHAPTER TWENTY-TWO

LATER, AFTER I'd stumbled down the stairs — my sense of balance was still dodgy, but getting better — we walked back to the carriages and rested in the shadow of one.

"You saved my life," I said softly.

"It was nothing," Sam said. "You'd have done the same for me."

"Probably," I said. "But I wasn't called upon to help. I wasn't the one who had to use his head and act coolly. You saved me, Sam. I owe you my life."

"Keep it," he laughed. "What would *I* do with it?"

"I'm serious, Sam. I owe you big-time. Anything you ever want or need, just ask, and I'll move heaven and earth to get it for you."

"You mean that?"

"Cross my heart," I swore.

"There is *one* thing," he said.

"Name it."

"I want to join the Cirque Du Freak."

"Saaaammmm ..." I groaned.

"You asked what I wanted, so I'm telling you," he replied.

"It's not that easy," I protested.

"Yes it is," he said. "You can talk to the owner and put in a good word for me. Come on, Darren, did you mean what you said or not?"

"All right," I sighed. "I'll ask Mr Tall."

"When?"

"Today," I promised. "As soon as I get back."

"All right!" Sam punched the air happily.

"But if he says no," I warned him, "that's the end of it, OK? I'll do what I can, but if Mr Tall says no, that *means* no."

"Sure," Sam said. "That's fine by me."

"Maybe there's a job for me, too," somebody said behind my back.

I spun around quickly, and there was R.V., smiling strangely.

"You shouldn't creep up on people like that," I snapped. "You gave me a fright."

"Sorry, man," R.V. said, but he didn't look very sorry.

"What are you doing out here?" Sam asked.

"I wanted to find Darren," R.V. said. "I never got a chance to thank him for my ticket."

"That's OK," I said. "I'm sorry I wasn't around to see you when it finished but I had business elsewhere."

"Sure," R.V. said, sitting down on the track beside me. "I can understand that. A show that size, there must be lots to do, huh? I bet they keep you real busy, right, man?"

"Right," I said.

R.V. beamed at the two of us. There was something about the way he was smiling that made me uneasy. It wasn't a nice smile.

"Tell me," R.V. said, "how's the Wolf Man doing?"

"He's fine," I said.

"He's chained up all the time, isn't he?" R.V. asked.

"No," I said, remembering Evra's warning.

"Isn't he?" R.V. acted surprised. "A wild beast like him, savage and dangerous, and he isn't locked up?"

"He's not really dangerous," I said. "That's an act. He's pretty tame actually." I could see Sam staring at me. He knew how wild the Wolf Man was and couldn't understand why I was lying.

"Tell me, man, what does a thing like that eat?" R.V. asked.

"Steak. Pork chops. Sausages." I forced a smile. "The usual stuff. All store-bought."

"Really? What about the goat that spider bit? Who eats that?"

"I don't know."

"Evra said the two of you bought the goat from a local farmer. Did it cost much?"

"Not really," I said. "It was quite sick, so it—"

I stopped. Evra had told R.V. we bought the goat from a *butcher*, not a farmer.

"I've been doing a spot of investigating, man," R.V. said softly. "Everybody else in my camp has been busy getting ready to move on but I've been walking around, counting sheep and cows, asking questions, digging for bones.

"Animals have been vanishing," R.V. continued. "The farmers aren't taking much notice – they don't mind the odd one or two going missing – but it fascinates me. Who do you think could be taking them, man?"

I didn't answer.

"Another thing," he said. "I was strolling along the river you're camped by, and do you know what I found downstream? Lots of small bones and scraps of skin and meat. Where do you think they could have come from, Darren?"

"I don't know," I said. Then I stood up. "I have to be going now. I'm expected back at the Cirque. Jobs to do."

"Don't let me keep you," R.V. smiled.

"When are you breaking camp?" I asked. "I might pop over to say goodbye before you leave."

"That's nice of you," R.V. said. "But don't worry, man. I won't be going anywhere soon."

I frowned. "I thought you said you were moving on."

"NOP are moving on," he said. "In fact they've already moved. They pulled out yesterday evening." He smiled icily. "But *I'm* staying a while longer. There are a few things I want to check out."

"Oh." Inside my head I cursed loudly, but outside I pretended to be happy. "That's good news. Well, see you around."

"Oh yes," R.V. said. "You'll see me around, man. You can bet on that. You'll be seeing *plenty* of me."

I grinned awkwardly.

"So long for now," I said.

"So long," R.V. replied.

"Wait up," Sam called. "I'll come with you."

"No," I said. "Come tomorrow. I'll have an answer from Mr Tall for you by then. Bye."

I took off before either of them could say anything else.

R.V.'s interest in the disappearance of the animals worried me at first, but as I walked back to camp I began to relax. When all was said and done, he was only a hairy harmless human, while those of us in the Cirque Du Freak were strange, powerful beings. What could he possibly do to hurt us?

CHAPTER TWENTY-THREE

I MEANT to report straight to Mr Tall when I got back, to tell him about R.V., but as I was heading for his van, Truska — the lady who was able to grow an incredible beard — grabbed my arm and made signs that she wanted me to follow her.

She led me to her tent. It was decorated more fancifully than most of the other tents and vans. The walls were covered with mirrors and paintings. There were huge wardrobes and dressing tables, and an enormous four-poster bed.

Truska said something in her strange seal-like voice, then stood me in the centre of the room and made a sign that I wasn't to move. She fetched a measuring tape and measured my body.

When she'd finished, she pursed her lips and thought for a few seconds, then clicked her fingers and hurried to one of the wardrobes. She rooted through it, emerging with a pair of trousers. She found a shirt in another wardrobe, a jacket in another, and a pair of shoes in a large chest. She let me pick my own vest, underpants and socks from one of the dressing-table drawers.

I stepped behind a silk screen to dress. Evra must have told her about my wish to find new clothes. It was a good job he had, as I probably would have kept on forgetting.

Truska clapped her hands when I came out and quickly pushed me in front of a mirror. The clothes fitted perfectly and, much to my surprise, I looked super-cool! The shirt was a light green colour, the trousers were dark purple, while the jacket was gold and blue. Truska found a long length of red satin cloth and wrapped it round my middle and that completed the picture: I looked just like a pirate!

"This is great!" I told her. "The only thing is," I said, pointing at my feet, "the shoes are a bit tight."

Truska took back the shoes and found a new pair. These were softer than the first and the toes curled up like Sinbad the Sailor's. I took an immediate shine to them.

"Thanks, Truska," I said, and started to leave. She raised a hand and I stopped. She pulled a chair over to one of the taller wardrobes and stood on it, reached up and brought down a huge round box. She plopped it on the floor, opened it, and pulled out a small brown hat with a feather in it, the sort that Robin Hood might have worn.

Before I could put the hat on, she made me sit down, got a pair of scissors and gave me a haircut, which I badly needed.

The haircut and hat were the icing on the cake. I almost didn't recognize myself in the mirror when I looked this time.

"Oh, Truska," I said. "I ... I ..." I couldn't find the words, so instead I threw my arms around her and gave her a big, sloppy kiss. I felt embarrassed when I let go, and was glad none of my friends had been around to see, but Truska was beaming.

I rushed off to show Evra my new look. He thought the clothes were great but swore he'd never asked Truska to help me. He said she must have either got sick of seeing me look so scruffy, or Mr Crepsley had asked her to fix me up, or she'd done it because she fancied me.

"She does not fancy me!" I shouted.

"Truska loves Darren," he sang. "Truska loves Darren."

"Oh, shut up, you slimy excuse for a reptile," I growled.

He laughed, not offended in the slightest.

"Darren and Truska sitting in a tree," he sang, "k-i-s-s-i-n-g. First comes love, then comes marriage, then comes Darren with the vampire carriage."

I gave a roar, jumped on him, wrestled him to the ground and wouldn't let go until he cried for mercy.

When we were finished, Evra went back to looking after his snake, while I went outside and got on with the day's jobs. I was on the go non-stop because I had to cover for Evra and do the work of two. With all that coming and going, and the excitement of having new clothes, I plain forgot about R.V. and telling Mr Tall about the eco warrior's threat to investigate the disappearing animals.

If I hadn't been so absent-minded, maybe things would have turned out differently, and perhaps our stay wouldn't have ended in bloodshed and tears.

CHAPTER TWENTY-FOUR

I WAS ready to drop by the time night came. The activity had worn me out. Evra had warned me not to sleep in his tent tonight; his snake was in a foul mood because of the virus and might bite. So I headed for Mr Crepsley's tent and made a bed on the floor beside Madam Octa's cage.

I fell asleep within a couple of minutes of lying down.

Some time later, as I was dreaming, something caught in my throat and made me gag. I coughed and awoke.

There was a figure above me, holding a small bottle to my mouth, trying to force a liquid down me. My first strange terrified thought was: "It's Mr Tiny!"

I bit the top off the bottle, cutting my lips, spilling most of the liquid. The man cursed, grabbed my chin and prised my gums apart. He tried pouring the last of the liquid into my open mouth, but I spat it out.

The man cursed again, then let go and slumped back. As my heartbeat slowed, I saw that it wasn't Mr Tiny.

It was Mr Crepsley.

"What the hell were you trying to do?" I screamed angrily. I was too mad to feel the pain in my cut lips.

He showed me the remains of the small bottle ... one of the containers he used to store human blood.

"You were trying to get me to drink!" I gasped.

"You have to," Mr Crepsley said. "You are wasting away, Darren. If you go on like this, you will be dead within a week. If you do not have the courage to drink, it must be forced into you."

I stared at him savagely. He looked uncomfortable and turned his eyes away from mine.

"I was trying to help," he said.

"If you ever try that again," I said slowly, "I'll kill you. I'll wait until day, then creep in and chop your head off."

He could tell I was serious, because he nodded glumly.

"Never again," he agreed. "I knew it would not work, but I had to try. If you had swallowed even a little, it would have kept you going a while longer, and once you had the taste, you might not be so afraid to drink again."

"I'll never have the taste!" I roared. "I won't drink human blood. I don't care if I *do* die. I won't drink it."

"Very well," he sighed. "I have done my best. If you insist on being stupid, on your own head be it."

"I'm not being stupid ... I'm being *human*," I growled.

"But you are not human," he said softly.

"I know," I replied. "But I want to be. I want to be like Sam. I want a family and ordinary friends. I want to grow old at the usual rate. I don't want to spend my life drinking blood and feeding off humans, worrying about sunlight and vampire hunters."

"Too bad," Mr Crepsley said. "It is the hand you have been dealt."

"I hate you," I snarled.

"Too bad," he said again. "You are stuck with me. If it is any compensation," he added, "I am none too fond of you either.

Turning you into a half-vampire was the worst mistake I ever made."

"So why not free me?" I wailed.

"I cannot," he said. "I would if I could. Of course, you are free to leave any time you like."

I stared at him suspiciously. "Really?" I asked.

"Really," he said. "I do not mind. In fact, I would prefer it if you did. That way, you would no longer be my responsibility. I would not have to watch you die."

I shook my head slowly. "I don't understand you at all," I said.

He smiled, almost tenderly. "Nor I you," he said.

We laughed a little then and things returned to normal. I didn't like what Mr Crepsley had tried, but understood why he'd tried it. You can't really hate someone who has your best interests at heart.

I told him what I'd done that day, about going to the railway yard with Sam and how he saved my life. I also told him about almost becoming Sam's blood-brother.

"It is a good job you stopped when you did," Mr Crepsley said.

"What would have happened if I hadn't?" I asked.

"Your blood would have tainted his. He would have developed a taste for raw meat. He would have hung around butcher shops, staring in the windows. He would have aged at a slightly slower rate than normal. It would not have been much of a difference, but it would have been enough."

"Enough to do what?" I asked.

"Drive him mad," Mr Crepsley said. "He would not have understood what was happening. He would have thought he was evil. He would not have known why his life had changed. Within ten years he would have been a screaming wreck."

I shivered at the thought of how close I'd come to destroying

Sam's life. This sort of thing was precisely why I had to stay with Mr Crepsley, until I'd learned everything about being a half-vampire.

"What do you think of Sam?" I asked.

"I have not seen much of him," Mr Crepsley said. "He comes mostly by day. But he seems nice. Very bright."

"He's been helping Evra and me with our chores," I said.

"I know."

"He's a good worker."

"So I have heard."

I licked my lips nervously. "He wants to join the Cirque," I said. Mr Crepsley's face darkened. "I was going to ask Mr Tall, but I forgot. I'll ask tomorrow. What do you think he'll say?"

"He will say you have to ask *me*. Children cannot join the Cirque Du Freak unless an independent member agrees to be their guardian."

"*I* could be his guardian," I said.

"You are not old enough. It would have to be me. I would have to give my permission. But I will not."

"Why?" I asked.

"Because it is a crazy idea," he said. "One child is bad enough. There is no way I would take on a second. Besides, he is human. I am stuck with you because of the vampire blood in your veins. Why should I put my neck on the line for a human?"

"He's my friend," I said. "He'd be company for me."

Mr Crepsley snorted. "Madam Octa is company enough."

"That's not the same," I whined.

"Tell me this," Mr Crepsley mused. "What happens when he finds out you are a vampire? You think he will understand? You think he will sleep easily, knowing his best friend would like nothing better than to slit his throat open and drink him dry?"

"I wouldn't do that!" I yelled.

127

"I know," Mr Crepsley agreed. "But I am a vampire. I know what you are really like. So does Mr Tall, Evra and the others. But how do you think an ordinary human would see you?"

I sighed unhappily. "You won't let him join?"

Mr Crepsley began to shake his head, then stopped and nodded slowly. "Very well," he said. "He can join."

"He *can*?" I stared at him, shocked. Even though I'd been arguing on Sam's behalf, I'd never really thought they would let him join.

"Yes," Mr Crepsley said. "He can join and travel with us and help you and Evra with your jobs. But on one condition." Mr Crepsley leant in close to me and treated me to his wickedest grin. "*He has to become a half-vampire too!*" he hissed.

CHAPTER TWENTY-FIVE

My heart was heavy when I saw Sam trot into camp early the next morning. I hated having to disappoint him, but knew I had to. There was no way I could let Mr Crepsley turn Sam into a half-vampire.

I'd thought about it a lot during the night, and the frightening thing was, I believed Sam would agree to become a half-vampire if I gave him the option. Smart as he was, I don't think he'd have stopped to consider the loneliness and awfulness of being a vampire.

He rushed over when he saw me, too excited to take any notice of my change of costume and hair cut.

"Did you ask him? Did you?" His face was bright, filled with hope.

"Yes," I said, smiling sadly.

"And?"

I shook my head. "Sorry, Sam. He said no."

Sam's face fell about a thousand kilometres.

"*Why?*" he shouted.

"You're too young," I said.

"You're not much older!" he snapped.

"But I have no parents," I lied. "I had no home to call my own when I joined the Cirque."

"I don't care about my parents," he sniffed.

"That's not true," I said. "You'd miss them."

"I could go home for holidays."

"It wouldn't work. You're not cut out for life in the Cirque Du Freak. Maybe later, when you're older."

"I don't care about 'later'!" he yelled. "I want to join *now*. I've worked hard. I've proved myself. I kept quiet when you were lying to R.V. about the Wolf Man yesterday. Did you tell that to Mr Tall?"

"I told him everything," I sighed.

"I don't believe you," Sam said. "I don't think you spoke to him at all. I want to see him myself."

I shrugged and pointed towards Mr Tall's van. "That's where you'll find him," I said.

Sam set off in a huff but slowed after a few steps, then came to a halt. He stubbed the ground miserably with his toes, then returned and sat down beside me.

"It's not fair," he grumbled. I could see tears trickling down his cheeks. "I'd made up my mind to join. It was going to be great. I had it all planned."

"There'll be other chances," I said.

"When?" he asked. "I've never heard of a freak-show playing round here before. When will I run into one again?"

I didn't answer.

"You wouldn't have liked it anyway," I said. "It's not as much fun as you think. Imagine what it's like in the middle of winter, when you have to get up at five in the morning and wash in ice-cold water and work outside in freezing blizzards."

"That doesn't bother me," Sam insisted. Then his tears stopped and he got a crafty look in his eyes. "Maybe I'll come along anyway," he said. "Maybe I'll sneak into one of the vans and stow away with you. Mr Tall would have to take me then."

"You can't do that!" I snapped. "You mustn't!"

"I will if I want," he grinned. "You can't stop me."

"I can," I growled.

"How?" he sneered.

I took a deep breath. The time had come to frighten Sam Grest away for ever. I couldn't tell him the truth about me, but I could invent a story almost as frightening, one guaranteed to send him running.

"I never told you what happened to my parents, did I, Sam? Or how I came to join the freak-show?" I kept my voice low and steady.

"No," Sam said quietly. "I often wondered but didn't want to ask."

"I killed them, Sam," I said.

"*What?*" His face went white.

"I go crazy sometimes. Like the Wolf Man. Nobody knows when it's going to happen, or why. I was in a hospital when I was younger but I seemed to be getting better. My parents brought me home for Christmas. After dinner, while I was pulling a cracker with Dad, I flipped.

"I tore him to pieces. Mum tried to drag me off but I killed her too. My little sister ran for help but I caught her. I ripped her apart the same way I'd ripped the cracker in two.

"Then, after I'd killed them ..." I locked eyes with Sam. It had to be a good act to make him believe. "*I ate them.*"

He stared at me, stunned.

"That's not true," he whispered. "It can't be."

"I killed and ate them, then ran away," I lied. "I was discovered by Mr Tall, who agreed to hide me. They have a special cage built to keep me in when I go mad. The problem is, nobody knows when it's going to happen. That's why most people avoid me.

Evra's OK because he's strong. So are some of the other performers. But ordinary humans ... I could kill them in the blink of an eye."

"You're lying," Sam said.

I picked up a large stick which was lying nearby, turned it round in my hands, then put it in my mouth and bit through it as if it was a big carrot.

"I'd chew your bones and spit you out as gristle," I told Sam. I'd cut my lips on the stick and the blood made me look a fright. "You wouldn't be able to stop me. You'd be sleeping in my tent if you joined the show and would be the one I'd go for first.

"You can't join the Cirque Du Freak," I said. "I wish you could – I'd love to have a friend – but it's not possible. I'd end up killing you if you joined."

Sam tried responding but couldn't get his mouth to work. He believed my far-fetched tale. He'd seen enough of the show to know that such things *could* happen here.

"Go away, Sam," I said sadly. "Go away and don't ever come back. It's safer this way. It's better. For both of us."

"Darren, I ... I ..." His head shook uncertainly.

"*Go!*" I roared, and pounded the ground with my hands. I bared my teeth and growled. I was able to make my voice much deeper than a human's, so it sounded like a wild animal.

Sam yelped, scrambled to his feet and sprinted for the cover of the trees, never once looking back.

I watched him go, heavy-hearted, certain my ploy had worked. He would never be back. I would see him no more. Our paths had separated and we would never meet again.

If I'd known how wrong I was – if I'd had any idea of the dreadful night which lay ahead – I'd have sped off after him and never returned to that foul circus of blood, that dreadful circus of *death*.

CHAPTER TWENTY-SIX

I WAS moping around when one of the Little People tapped me on the back. It was the one with the limp.

"What do you want?" I asked.

The tiny man — if it was a man — in the blue-hooded robes rubbed his belly with his hands. This was the sign that he and his brothers were hungry.

"You just had breakfast," I said.

He rubbed his belly again.

"It's too early for dinner."

He rubbed his belly again.

I knew that this would go on for hours if I let it. He would patiently follow me around, rubbing his belly, until I agreed to go and hunt for him.

"All right," I snapped. "I'll see what I can find. But I'm on my own today, so if I don't come back with a full bag: tough."

He rubbed his belly again.

I snorted and set off.

I shouldn't have gone hunting. I was very weak. I could still run quicker than a human and I was stronger than most kids my age, but I wasn't super-fit or extra-strong any longer. Mr Crepsley had said I would be dead within a week if I didn't drink human blood, and I knew he'd spoken the truth. I could feel myself wasting away. A few more days and I wouldn't be able to pull myself out of bed.

I tried catching a rabbit but wasn't fast enough. I worked up a sweat chasing it and had to sit down for a few minutes. Next, I went looking for road-kill, but couldn't find any dead animals. Finally, because I was tired and half-afraid of what would happen if I returned to camp empty-handed (the Little People might decide to eat *me!*), I headed for a field full of sheep.

They were grazing peacefully when I arrived. They were used to humans and barely lifted their heads when I entered the field and walked among them.

I was looking for an old sheep, or one that looked sick. That way I needn't feel so lousy about killing it. I eventually found one with skinny, trembling legs and a dazed expression, and decided she'd do. She looked as though she hadn't long to live anyway.

If I'd had my full powers, I'd have snapped her neck and she would have been dead in an instant, without any pain. But I was weak and clumsy, and didn't twist hard enough the first time.

The sheep began to bleat with agony.

She tried running away but her legs wouldn't carry her. She fell to the ground, where she lay, bleating unhappily.

I tried breaking her neck again but couldn't. In the end I fetched a stone and finished the job. It was a messy, horrible way to kill an animal and I felt ashamed of myself as I grabbed its back legs and hauled it away from the flock.

I'd almost reached the fence before I realized somebody was sitting on top of it, waiting for me. I dropped the sheep and looked up, expecting an angry farmer.

But it wasn't a farmer.

It was R.V.

And he was mad as hell.

"How could you?" he shouted. "How could you kill a poor, innocent animal in so cruel a manner?"

"I tried killing her quickly," I said. "I tried snapping her neck, but I couldn't. I'd have left her when I failed, but she was in pain. I thought it was better to finish her off than leave her to suffer."

"That's real big of you, man," he said sarcastically. "Do you think you'll get the Nobel Peace Prize for that?"

"Please, R.V.," I said. "Don't be angry. She was sick. The farmer would have killed her anyway. Even if she'd lived she would have been sent to a butcher's in the end."

"That don't make it right," he said angrily. "Just because other people are nasty, it don't mean you should be nasty too."

"Killing animals isn't nasty," I said. "Not when it's for food."

"What's wrong with vegetables?" he asked. "We don't need to eat meat, man. We don't need to kill."

"*Some* people need meat," I disagreed. "Some can't live without it."

"Then they should be left to die!" R.V. roared. "That sheep never did any harm to anyone. As far as I'm concerned, killing her is worse than killing a human. You're a murderer, Darren Shan."

I shook my head sadly. There was no point arguing with somebody this stubborn. R.V. had his way of looking at the world, while I had mine.

"Look, R.V.," I said, "I don't enjoy killing. I'd be over the moon if everyone in the world was a vegetarian. But they're not. People eat meat and that's a fact of life. I'm only doing what I have to."

"Well, we'll see what the police have to say about it," R.V. said.

"The police?" I frowned. "What do they have to do with it?"

"You've killed somebody else's sheep," he laughed cruelly. "Do you think they'll let you get away with that? They won't arrest you for murdering rabbits and foxes – more's the pity – but they'll charge you for killing a sheep. I'll have the police and health inspectors down on you like a tonne of bricks," he grinned.

"You won't!" I gasped. "You don't like the police. You're always fighting against them."

"When I have to," he agreed. "But when I can get them on my side ..." He laughed again. "They'll arrest you first, then turn your camp upside-down. I've been studying the goings-on there. I've seen the way you treat that poor hairy man."

"The Wolf Man?"

"Yes. You keep him locked away like an animal."

"He *is* an animal," I said.

"No," R.V. disagreed. "*You* are the animal, man."

"R.V., listen," I said. "We don't have to be enemies. Come back to camp with me. Talk to Mr Tall and the others. See how we live. Get to know and understand us. There's no need to—"

"Save it," he snapped. "I'm going for the police. Nothing you can say will stop me."

I took a deep breath. I liked R.V. but knew I couldn't allow him to destroy the Cirque Du Freak.

"Very well," I said. "If nothing I *say* can stop you, maybe you'll respond to something I *do*."

Summoning all my remaining strength, I threw the dead body of the sheep at R.V. It struck him in the chest and knocked him flying from the fence. He yelled with surprise, then with pain as he landed heavily on the ground.

I leapt over the fence and was on him before he could move.

"How did you do that, man?" he gasped.

"Never mind," I snapped.

"Kids can't throw sheep," he said. "How did—"

"Shut up!" I shouted and slapped his bearded face. He stared up at me, shocked. "Listen, Reggie Veggie," I growled, using the name he hated, "and listen well. You *won't* go to the police or the health people. Because, if you do, the sheep won't be the only dead body I drag back to the Cirque Du Freak today."

"What are you?" he asked. His voice was trembling and his eyes were filled with terror.

"I'm the end of you if you cross me," I swore, then dug my fingernails into the soil at either side of his face and squeezed his head between my hands, just enough to let him know how strong I was.

"Get out of here, Reggie," I said. "Go and find your friends in NOP. Stick to protesting against new roads and bridges. You're in over your head here. Me and my friends in the Cirque are freaks, and freaks don't obey the same laws as other people. Understand?"

"You're crazy," he said softly.

"Yes," I sighed. "But not as crazy as you'll be if you stay and interfere."

I stood and draped the sheep over my shoulders.

"Going to the police would be useless anyway," I said. "By the time they reach the camp, this sheep would be long gone, bones and all.

"You can do what you like, R.V. Stay or go. Report me to the police or keep your mouth shut. It's up to you. All I've left to say is this: to me and my kind, you're no different than this sheep." I gave it a shake. "We'd think no more of killing you than we would any dumb animal of the fields."

"You're a monster!" R.V. gasped.

"Yes," I agreed. "But I'm only a *baby* monster. You should see what some of the others are like." I smiled nastily at him, hating myself for acting so meanly, but knowing this was the way it had to be. "So long, Reggie Veggie," I said, and walked away.

I didn't look back. I didn't need to. I could hear the chattering of his terrified teeth practically all the way back to camp.

CHAPTER TWENTY-SEVEN

THIS TIME I went straight to Mr Tall and told him about R.V. He listened carefully, then said, "You handled him well."

"I did what I had to," I replied. "I'm not proud of it. I don't like bullying or scaring people, but there was no other way."

"By rights, you should have killed him," Mr Tall said. "That way, he could do us no harm whatsoever."

"I'm not a murderer," I told him.

"I know," he sighed. "Nor am I. It's a pity one of the Little People wasn't with you. They'd have chopped his head off without a second's hesitation."

"What do you think we should do?" I asked.

"I don't think he can cause many problems," Mr Tall mused. "He'll probably be too scared to go to the police straightaway. Even if he does, there's no evidence against you. It would be an unwanted complication, but we've had plenty of dealings with officers of the law in the past. We could cope.

"The health authorities worry me more. We could hit the road and lose them, but people in the health department tend to trail you around like hound-dogs once they've got your scent.

"We'll leave tomorrow," he decided. "There's a show

scheduled for tonight and I hate cancelling on short notice. Dawn is the earliest any health inspector could be here, so we'll break camp before then."

"You're not angry with me?" I asked.

"No," he said. "This isn't the first time we've clashed with the public. You're not to blame."

I helped Mr Tall spread the word of our departure among the camp. Everybody took it in their stride. Most seemed happy to be getting this much notice; they often had to move on with only an hour or two of warning.

It was another busy day for me. As well as preparing for the show, I had to help people get ready for leaving. I offered to help Truska pack her belongings, but her tent was already bare when I got there. She only winked when I asked how she'd packed so quickly.

I told Mr Crepsley about our morning departure when he awoke. He didn't seem surprised.

"We have been here long enough," he said.

I asked to be left out of that night's show because I wasn't feeling very well.

"I'll get to bed early," I said, "and have a long sleep."

"It will not do any good," Mr Crepsley warned. "There is only one thing that will make you feel better, and you know what it is."

Night rolled on, and soon it was time for the show to begin. There was another big crowd. The roads were blocked with cars in both directions. Everybody in the Cirque was busy, either preparing to go on stage, or getting people seated, or selling stuff.

The only two who seemed to have nothing to do were me and Evra, who wasn't performing because of his ill snake. He left her for a few minutes to watch the start of the show. We stood to one side of the stage as Mr Tall got the ball rolling and introduced the Wolf Man.

We stuck around until the first break, then strolled outside and studied the stars.

"I'll miss this place when we move on," Evra said. "I like the countryside. You can't see stars so well in a city."

"I didn't know you were interested in astronomy," I said.

"I'm not," he replied. "But I enjoy looking up at the stars."

I got dizzy after a while and had to sit down.

"You're not feeling too good, are you?" Evra asked.

I smiled weakly. "I've been better."

"Still not drinking human blood?" I shook my head. He sat beside me. "You've never told me *exactly* why you won't drink it," he said. "Surely it can't be so different to animal blood?"

"I don't know," I said. "And I don't want to find out." I paused. "I'm afraid that if I drink human blood, I'll be *evil*. Mr Crepsley says vampires aren't evil but I think they are. I think anyone who looks at humans as if they're animals *must* be evil."

"But if it's to keep you alive ..." Evra said.

"That's how it would start," I said. "I'd tell myself I was doing it to keep going. I'd swear never to drink more than I needed. But what if I couldn't stop myself? I'll need more as I grow older and larger. What if I can't control my thirst? What if I kill someone?"

"I don't think you could," Evra said. "You're *not* evil, Darren. I don't think a good person can do evil things. As long as you treat human blood like medicine, you'll be all right."

"Maybe," I said, though I didn't believe it. "Anyway, I'm OK for the time being. I don't have to make a final decision for a couple more days."

"Would you really let yourself die rather than drink?" Evra asked.

"I don't know," I answered honestly.

"I'd miss you if you died," Evra said sadly.

"Well," I said uncomfortably, "maybe it won't come to that. Maybe there's some other way I can survive, a way that Mr Crepsley doesn't want to tell me about until he has no other choice."

Evra grunted. He knew as well as me that there was no other way.

"I'm going to check on my snake," he said. "Do you want to come and sit with us a while?"

"No," I said. "I'd better get some sleep. We'll have to rise early and I'm exhausted."

We said our goodnights and parted. I didn't head straight for Mr Crepsley's tent, but wandered through the camp-site, thinking about my conversation with Evra, wondering what it would feel like to die. I'd "died" once before, and been buried, but that wasn't the same thing. If I died for real, I'd be dead for good. Life would be over, my body would decay, and then ...

I glanced up at the stars. Was *that* where I'd be heading? To the other side of the universe? Vampire Paradise?

It was a troubling time. When I was living at home I'd hardly ever thought about death; it was something that only happened to old people. Now here I was, almost face to face with it.

If only somebody else could decide for me. I should be worrying about school and making the local football team, not about whether I should drink human blood or let myself die. It wasn't fair. I was too young. I shouldn't have to—

I saw a shadow passing the front of a nearby tent but took little notice of it. It wasn't until I heard a sharp snapping sound that I wondered who it might have been. Nobody should be out here. Everyone involved with the show was in the big tent. Was it somebody from the audience?

I decided to investigate.

I headed in the direction that the shadow had taken. It was a dark night and after a few turns I couldn't figure out which way the person had gone. I was on the verge of abandoning the search when I heard another sharp snapping sound, closer this time.

A quick look around convinced me of my location, and I knew immediately where the sounds must have come from: *the Wolf Man's cage!*

Taking a deep breath to steady my nerves, I put my best foot forward and hurried to check it out.

CHAPTER TWENTY-EIGHT

THE GRASS was damp, so it bent beneath my feet and made no sound. When I reached the last caravan before the Wolf Man's cage, I paused and listened.

There was a soft jangling sound, as though heavy chains were being lightly shaken.

I stepped out from under cover.

There were dim lights at either side of the Wolf Man's cage, so I was able to see everything in perfect detail. He'd been wheeled back here after his act, as he was every night. There was a slab of meat in his cage, which normally he'd be feasting on. But not tonight. Tonight he was focused on something different.

There was a large man in front of the Wolf Man's cage. He had a huge pair of pliers with him and had cut some of the chains which were holding the door shut.

The man was trying to unwrap the chains but wasn't enjoying much success. He cursed softly to himself and lifted the pliers to cut through another link.

"What are you doing?" I shouted.

The man jumped with shock, dropped the pliers and spun around.

It was, as I had guessed, R.V.

He looked guilty and scared at first, but when he saw I was alone he grew in confidence.

"Stay back!" he warned.

"What are you doing?" I asked again.

"Freeing this poor abused creature," he said. "I wouldn't keep the wildest of animals in a cage like this. It's inhuman. I'm letting him go. I rang the police — they'll be out here in the morning — but I decided to do a bit of work of my own beforehand."

"You can't do that!" I gasped. "Are you crazy? That guy's savage. He'd kill everything within a five-kilometre radius if you let him out!"

"So *you* say," R.V. sneered. "I don't believe that. It's been my experience that animals react according to how they're treated. If you treat them like mad monsters, they'll act that way. If, on the other hand, you treat them with respect, love and humanity ..."

"You don't know what you're doing," I told him. "The Wolf Man isn't like other animals. Come away from there before you do any real damage. We can talk this over. We can—"

"No!" he screamed. "I'm through talking!"

He spun back to the chains and began struggling with them again. He reached into the cage and tugged the thickest chains through the bars. The Wolf Man watched him silently.

"R.V., stop!" I shouted and raced over to prevent him opening the door. I grabbed his shoulders and tried pulling him away but I wasn't strong enough. I punched him in the ribs a few times but he only grunted and doubled his efforts.

I grabbed for his hands, to prise them off the chains, but the bars were in the way.

"Leave me alone!" R.V. yelled. He turned his head to address me directly. His eyes were wild. "You won't stop me!" he screeched. "You won't prevent me from doing my duty. I'll free this victim. I'll see justice done. I'll—"

He stopped ranting all of a sudden. His face turned deathly white and his body shuddered, then went stiff.

There was a crunching, munching, ripping sound, and when I looked inside the cage, I realized the Wolf Man had made his move.

He'd sprung across the cage while we were arguing, grabbed both of R.V.'s arms, jammed them in his mouth and *bitten them off beneath the elbows!*

R.V. fell away from the cage, shocked. He lifted his shortened arms and watched as blood pumped from the holes at the ends of his elbows.

I tried snatching his lower arms back from the mouth of the Wolf Man – if I could retrieve them, they could be stuck back on – but he moved too quickly for me, leapt back out of reach and began chewing. Within seconds the arms were a mess and I knew they'd be no good ever again.

"Where are my hands?" R.V. asked.

I switched my attention back to the bearded man. He was staring at the stumps that were his arms, a funny look on his face, not yet feeling the pain that must surely come.

"Where are my hands?" he asked again. "They're gone. They were there a minute ago. Where did all this blood come from? Why can I see the bone inside my skin?

"*Where are my hands?*" He screamed this last question at the top of his voice.

"You have to come with me," I said, drawing near. "We have to get your arms seen to, before you bleed to death."

"Stay away from me!" R.V. yelled. He tried raising a hand to shove me back, then remembered he didn't have hands any more.

"You're responsible for this!" he shouted. "You did this to me!"

"No, R.V., it was the Wolf Man," I said, but he wasn't listening.

"This is your fault," he insisted. "You took my hands. You're an evil little monster and you stole my hands. My hands! My hands!"

He began screaming again. I reached for him but this time he brushed me aside, turned and ran. He tore screaming through the camp, his blood-drenched half-arms raised high above his head, yelling as loudly as he could, until he vanished into the night.

"My hands! My hands! My hands!"

I wanted to run after him, but was afraid he might attack me. I set off to find Mr Crepsley and Mr Tall – they'd know what to do – but was stopped dead in my tracks by a worrying growl behind me.

I turned slowly. The Wolf Man was at the door of the cage, which was swinging wide open! He'd somehow removed the last of the chains and freed himself.

I remained perfectly still as he stood and grinned viciously, his long, sharp teeth glinting in the dim light. He looked to the left and right, stretched out his hands and grabbed the bars to either side. Then he crouched down low and tensed his legs.

He sprang, propelling himself towards me.

I shut my eyes and waited for the end to come.

I heard and felt him land about a metre in front of me. I began to say my final prayers.

But then I heard him flying overhead and realized he'd bounced over me. For a couple of terrifying seconds I waited for his teeth to bite through the back of my neck and gnaw my head off.

But they didn't.

Confused, I turned, blinking. He was racing away from me! I glimpsed a figure ahead of him, running quickly between the caravans, and understood he was after somebody else. He'd

147

passed me up in favour of a tastier meal.

I took several stumbling steps after the departing Wolf Man. I was smiling and silently thanking the gods. I couldn't believe how close I'd come to death. When he'd leapt through the air, I was sure—

My feet struck something and I stopped.

I looked down and saw a bag. The person the Wolf Man was chasing must have dropped it, and for the first time I wondered who it was that the wild Wolf Man was after.

I picked up the bag. It was the sort you carry over one shoulder. It was full of clothes, which I could feel through the covers. A small jar fell out as I turned the bag around. Retrieving it, I thumbed up the lid and caught the bitter aroma of ... *pickled onions!*

My heart almost stopped. Furiously, I began searching for a name tag, praying the pickled onions didn't mean what I feared.

My prayers went unanswered.

The hand writing, when I found it, was neat, but unjoined. The writing of a child.

"This bag is the property of Sam Grest," it said, and his address was just beneath. "Hands off!!" it warned at the end, which was quite ironic given what had happened a minute or so earlier with R.V.

But I hadn't time to laugh at the dark joke.

Sam! For some reason he'd sneaked out here tonight – probably to stow away with the Cirque – and must have seen and followed me. It was Sam the Wolf Man's beady eyes had spotted, standing behind me. It was Sam running for his life through the camp.

The Wolf Man was after Sam!

CHAPTER TWENTY-NINE

I SHOULDN'T have pursued them on my own. I should have gone for help. It was madness, rushing off into the darkness by myself.

But he was after Sam. Sam, who wanted to join the Cirque. Sam, who asked to be my blood-brother. Harmless, friendly, long-winded Sam. The boy who'd saved my life.

I didn't think about my own safety. Sam was in trouble and there wasn't time to seek the help of others. It might prove the death of me but I had to go after them, to try and save Sam. I owed him.

I cleared the camp quickly. The clouds had parted overhead and I spotted the Wolf Man disappearing into the trees. I hurried after him, running as fast as I could.

I heard the Wolf Man howl a while later, which was a good sign. It meant he was still chasing Sam. If he'd caught him, he'd be too busy eating to howl.

I wondered why he hadn't caught him yet. He should have. Though I had never seen him running in the open, I was sure he must be fast. Perhaps he was playing with Sam, toying with him before he moved in for the kill.

Their footprints were clear in the damp night earth, but I

149

would have been able to follow from their sounds in any case. It's hard to run silently through a forest, especially at night.

We ran in that fashion for several minutes, Sam and the Wolf Man far in front and out of sight, me trailing behind. My legs were beginning to tire but I forced myself on.

I thought about what I would do when I caught up. There was no way I could beat the Wolf Man in a fair fight. Perhaps I could slam him over the head with a stick or something, but it was unlikely. He was strong and fast, and had the taste of human blood. He would be pretty much unstoppable.

The most I could hope to do was throw myself in his path and take Sam's place. If I offered myself instead of Sam, maybe he'd take me and Sam could escape.

I wouldn't mind dying for Sam. I'd given up my humanity for one friend; it wasn't asking so much more to give up my life for another.

Besides, this way, if I died, it would be for a good cause. I'd no longer have to worry about drinking human blood or starving to death. I could go down fighting.

After a few more minutes, I burst into a clearing and realized where Sam had led us: the old deserted railway station.

It showed he was still thinking clearly. This was the best place to come, with plenty of hiding spots and lots of stuff — chunks of metal and glass — to use in a fight. Maybe neither of us would have to die. Maybe there was a chance we could win this battle.

I saw the Wolf Man pause in the middle of the station yard and sniff the air. He howled again, a loud spine-shivering howl, then set off towards one of the rusty carriages.

I ran around the back of the carriage, moving as quietly as I could. I listened for sounds when I got there but couldn't hear anything. I lifted myself up and looked in one of the carriage windows: nothing.

I lowered myself and slid along to the third window over. Again, I could see nothing when I looked inside.

I was lifting myself to peep in the next window, when I glimpsed a metal bar moving towards my face at high speed.

I twisted aside just in time to avoid it. It whistled by the side of my face, scratching me but not doing any serious damage.

"Sam, stop, it's *me!*" I hissed, dropping to the ground. There was silence for a moment, then Sam's face appeared in the round window.

"Darren?" he asked. "What are you doing here?"

"I followed you," I said.

"I thought you were the Wolf Man. I was trying to kill you."

"You nearly did."

"I'm sorry."

"For God's sake, Sam, don't waste time apologizing," I snapped. "We're in big trouble. We have to put our thinking caps on. Get out here quick."

He retreated from the window. There were soft shuffling sounds, then he appeared out of the carriage door. He checked to make sure the Wolf Man wasn't around, jumped down and crept over to meet me.

"Where is he?" Sam asked.

"I don't know," I whispered. "He's around somewhere, though. I saw him coming in this direction."

"Maybe he found something else to attack," Sam suggested hopefully. "A sheep or a cow."

"I wouldn't bet on it," I grunted. "He wouldn't have run all this way, just to abandon the chase at the very end."

We huddled close together, Sam covering the right with his eyes, me the left. I could feel his body trembling and I'm sure he could feel mine shaking too.

"What are we going to do?" Sam asked.

"I don't know," I replied. "Any ideas?"

"A few," he said. "We could lead him into the guard's house. He might fall through the rotten floorboards. We could trap him down there."

"Maybe," I said. "But what if *we* fall through as well? We'd be trapped for sure. He could jump down and eat us whenever he liked."

"How about the rafters?" Sam asked. "We could climb out into the middle of a rafter and hang on, back to back. We could take clubs or sticks with us and beat him off if he attacked. There'd only be one way for him to come at us up there."

"And somebody's sure to arrive from the Cirque Du Freak sooner or later," I said, thinking it over. "But what if he decides to snap the rafter at one end?"

"They're set fairly deeply into brick," Sam said. "I don't think he could break them with his bare hands."

"Would a rafter hold the weight of three of us?" I asked.

"I'm not sure," Sam admitted. "But at least if we fell from that height it'd be over quickly. Who knows: we might get lucky and fall on the Wolf Man. He could cushion our fall and get killed in the process."

I laughed sickly. "You've been watching too many cartoons. But it's a good idea. Better than any I can think of. It won't be easy to fend him off, even on a rafter, but it will make it harder for him to get at us."

"How long do you think it'll be before the people from the Cirque get here?" Sam asked.

"Depends on when they realize what's happening," I said. "If we're lucky, they'll have heard him howling and might be here in a couple of minutes. Otherwise we might have to wait until the end of the show, which could be another hour, maybe longer."

"Do you have a weapon?" Sam asked.

"No," I said. "I didn't have time to pick anything up."

He handed me a short iron bar. "Here," he said. "I had this for back-up. It's not very good, but it's better than nothing."

"Any sign of the Wolf Man?" I asked.

"No," he said. "Not yet."

"We'd better get going before he arrives," I said, then paused. "How are we going to get to the station house? It's a long run and the Wolf Man could be hiding anywhere along the way."

"We'll have to race for it and hope for the best," Sam said.

"Will we split up?" I asked.

"I'd rather not," he said. "I think we're better off together."

"I agree. Are you ready to start?"

"Give me a few seconds," he said.

I turned and watched him breathing. His face was white and his clothes were torn and dirty from running through the woods, but he looked ready for business. He was a tough little character.

"Why did you come back tonight, Sam?" I asked softly.

"To join the Cirque Du Freak," he answered.

"Even after everything I told you about me?"

"I decided to risk it," he said. "I mean, you're a friend. We have to stick by our friends, don't we? Your story made me more determined to join, once I'd recovered from my initial fright. I might have been able to help you. I've read books about personality disorders. Maybe I could have cured you."

I couldn't help grinning. "You're a moron, Sam Grest," I said.

"I know," he smiled. "So are you. That's why we make a good pair."

"If we get out of this," I told him, "feel free to join up. And you don't have to worry about me eating you: that was just a story to frighten you off."

"Really?" he asked.

"Really," I said.

"Phew." He wiped his brow. "I can rest easy now."

"You can if the Wolf Man doesn't get us," I agreed. "Ready yet?"

"I'm ready." He hitched up his trousers and prepared to run. "On the count of three," he said.

"OK," I replied.

"One," he began.

We faced in the direction of the guard's house.

"Two."

We got into sprint-start positions.

"Thr—"

Before he could finish, a pair of hairy hands darted out from underneath the carriage, where — I realized too late — the Wolf Man was hiding. The fingers wrapped around Sam's lower legs, grabbed him by the ankles and dragged him down to the ground!

CHAPTER THIRTY

SAM STARTED to scream as soon as the hands tightened on his
ankles. The fall knocked the breath out of him, silencing him
momentarily, but after a second or two he was back screaming
again.

I fell to my knees, grabbed Sam's arms and pulled.

I could see the Wolf Man underneath the carriage, spread out on
his hairy belly, grinning wildly. Drool was dripping from his jaws.

I tugged hard and Sam slid towards me, but the Wolf Man
came with him, wriggling out from under the carriage, not
loosening his grip.

I stopped pulling and let go of Sam. I grabbed the long iron
bar which he'd dropped, jumped to my feet and began pounding
the outstretched arms of the Wolf Man, who howled angrily.

The Wolf Man released one of his hairy paws and swatted at
me. I ducked out of the way and struck at the hand still holding
Sam. The Wolf Man yelped with pain and the fingers came free.

"Run!" I screamed to Sam as I yanked him to his feet.

We set off towards the guard's house, side by side. I could
hear the Wolf Man scrabbling out from beneath the carriage.
He'd been playing with us before but now he was furious. I knew

he'd come at us with everything he had. The games were over. There was no way we'd make the shelter of the guard's house. He'd have us before we were halfway across the yard.

"Keep ... running," I gasped to Sam, then stopped and turned to meet the charge of the oncoming Wolf Man.

My actions took him by surprise and he ran into me. His body was hairy and sweaty and heavy. The collision sent both of us flying to the floor. Our arms and legs were all tangled up but I quickly freed myself and whacked him with the bar.

The Wolf Man roared angrily and swiped at my arm. This time he connected, just below where it joined with my shoulder. The force of the blow deadened my arm, which became a useless lump of flesh and bone. I dropped the bar, then reached for it with my good left hand.

But the Wolf Man was quicker. He snatched up the bar and tossed it far away, where it fell with a clang, lost to the darkness.

He stood slowly, grinning nastily. I could read the expression in his eyes and knew, if he could speak, he would be saying something like: "Now, Darren Shan, you're mine! You had your fun and games but now it's killing time!"

He grabbed my body by the sides, opened his mouth wide, and leant forward to bite my face off. I could smell the stench of his breath and see bits of meat and shirt from R.V.'s arms stuck between his yellowish teeth.

Before he could snap his jaws shut, something hit the side of his head and knocked him off-balance.

I glimpsed Sam behind him, a heavy chunk of wood in his hands. He hit the Wolf Man again, this time causing his hands to loosen.

"One good turn deserves another!" Sam yelled, slamming the wood into the Wolf Man for a third time. "Come on! We have to—"

I never heard Sam's next words. Because as I started towards him, the Wolf Man lashed out blindly with one of his fists. It was a wild shot but he got lucky and it slammed into my face, knocking me backwards.

My head almost exploded. I saw bright lights and huge stars, then slumped to the ground in a faint.

When I recovered a few seconds or minutes later – I'm not sure how much time had passed – the railway station was eerily quiet. I could hear nobody running or screaming or fighting. All I could hear was a steady munching sound, a little way ahead of me.

Munch. Munch. Munch.

I sat up slowly, ignoring the hammering pain in my head.

It took my eyes a few seconds to re-adjust to the darkness. When I could see again, I realized I was gazing at the back of the Wolf Man. He was crouched on all fours, head bent over something. *He* was the one making the munching sounds.

The dizziness from the punch meant it took me a while to realize it wasn't a some*thing* he was eating ... it was a some*one*.

SAM!!!

I scrambled to my feet, pain forgotten, and rushed forward, but one look at the bloody mess beneath the Wolf Man and I knew I was too late.

"*NO!*" I screamed and punched the Wolf Man with my one good hand, attacking senselessly.

He grunted and shoved me away. I sprang back and this time kicked as well as punched. He growled and tried shoving again, but I held on and pulled his hair and ears.

He howled then and finally lifted his mouth. It was red, a dark, dreadful red, full of guts and blood and bits of flesh and bone.

He rolled on top of me, forcing me down, and pinned me

with one long hairy arm. His head shot back and he howled up at the night sky. Then, with a demonic snarl, he drove his teeth towards my throat, meaning to finish me off with one quick bite.

CHAPTER THIRTY-ONE

AT ALMOST the last possible moment, a pair of hands appeared out of the darkness and grabbed the Wolf Man's jaw, halting his plunge.

The hands twisted the head to one side, causing the Wolf Man to shriek and fall off me.

His attacker climbed on to his back and held him down. I saw fists flying faster than my eyes could follow and then the Wolf Man was lying unconscious on the ground.

His attacker stood and pulled me to my feet. I found myself gazing up into the flushed, scarred face of Mr Crepsley.

"I came as soon as I could," the vampire gasped, turning my head gently to the left and right, examining the damage. "Evra heard the howls of the Wolf Man. He did not know about you and the boy. He just thought the creature had burst free.

"Evra told Mr Tall, who cancelled the rest of the show and organized a search party. Then I thought of *you*. When I saw your bed was empty, I scouted around and found your trail."

"I thought ... I was going to ... die," I moaned, finding it hard to speak. I was bruised all over and suffering from shock. "I was certain. I thought ... nobody would come. I ..."

I threw my good arm around Mr Crepsley and hugged him hard.

"Thank you," I sobbed. "Thank you. Thank you. Thank—"

I stopped, remembering my fallen friend.

"Sam!" I screamed. I let go of Mr Crepsley and rushed to where the boy was lying.

The Wolf Man had torn Sam's belly open and eaten a lot of his insides. Amazingly, Sam was still alive when I got to him. His eyelids were fluttering and he was breathing lightly.

"Sam, are you OK?" I asked. It was a stupid question, but the only one my battered lips could form. "Sam?" I brushed his forehead with my fingers but he showed no signs of hearing or feeling me. He looked quite peaceful, from the chest up at least.

Mr Crepsley knelt down beside me and checked the body.

"Can you save him?" I asked. He shook his head slowly. "You must!" I shouted. "You can close the wounds. We can call a doctor. You can give him a potion. There must be some way to—"

"Darren," he said softly, "there is nothing we can do. He is dying. The damage is too great. Another couple of minutes and ..." He sighed. "At least he is beyond feeling. There will be no pain."

"No!" I screamed and threw myself on to Sam. I was crying bitterly, sobbing so hard it hurt.

"Sam! You can't die! Sam! Stay alive! You can join the Cirque and travel with us all over the world. You can ... you ..."

I could say no more, only lower my head, cling to Sam, and weep.

In the deserted old railway yard, the Wolf Man lay unconscious to my rear. Mr Crepsley sat silently by my side. Beneath me, Sam Grest – who'd been my friend and saved my life – remained perfectly still and slipped further and further into the final sleep of an untimely, horrible death.

CHAPTER THIRTY-TWO

AFTER A while, I felt a slight tugging at the sleeve of my left arm. I looked around. Mr Crepsley was standing over me, looking miserable.

"Darren," he said, "it will not seem like the right time but there is something you must do. For Sam's sake. And your own."

"What are you talking about?" I wiped some of the tears from my face and stared up at him. "Can we save him? Tell me if we can. I'll do anything."

"There is nothing we can do to save his *body*," Mr Crepsley told me. "He is dying and nothing can change that. But there is something we can do for his *spirit*.

"Darren," he said, "*you must drink Sam's blood.*"

I went on staring at him, but now it was a stare of disbelief, not hope.

"How could you?" I asked softly. "One of my best friends is dying, and all you can think about ... You're sick! You're a sick, twisted monster. You should be dying, not Sam. I hate you. Get out of here."

"You do not understand," he said.

"Yes I do!" I screamed. "Sam's dying, but all you're worried

161

about is blooding me. Do you know what you are? You're a no-good—"

"Do you remember our discussion about vampires being able to absorb part of a person's spirit?" he asked.

I'd been about to call him something awful but his question confused me.

"What's that got to do with this?" I asked.

"Darren, this is important. Do you remember?"

"Yes," I said softly. "What about it?"

"Sam is dying," Mr Crepsley said. "A few more minutes and he will be gone. For ever. But you can keep part of him alive within you if you drink from him now and take his life before the wounds of the Wolf Man can."

I couldn't believe what I was hearing.

"You want *me* to kill Sam?" I screamed.

"No," he sighed. "Sam has already been killed. But if you finish him off before he dies from the bites of the Wolf Man, you will save some of his memories and feelings. In you he can live on."

I shook my head. "I can't drink his blood," I whispered. "Not Sam's." I glanced down at the small, savaged body. "I can't."

Mr Crepsley sighed. "I will not force you to," he said. "But think carefully about it. What happened tonight is a tragedy which will haunt you for a very long time, but if you drink from Sam and absorb part of his essence, dealing with his death will be easier. Losing a loved one is hard. This way, you need not lose all of him."

"I can't drink from him," I sobbed. "He was my friend."

"It is *because* he was your friend that you must," Mr Crepsley said, then turned away and left me to decide.

I stared down at Sam. He looked so lifeless, as though he'd already lost that which made him human, alive, unique. I thought of his jokes and long words and hopes and dreams, and how awful it would be if all of that simply vanished with his passing.

Kneeling, I placed the fingers of my left hand on Sam's red neck. "I'm sorry, Sam," I moaned, then dug my sharp nails into his soft flesh, leant forward and stuck my mouth over the holes they'd made.

Blood gushed in and made me gag. I nearly fell away, but with an effort I held my place and gulped it down. His blood was hot and salty and ran down my throat like thick creamy butter.

Sam's pulse slowed as I drank, then stopped. But I went on drinking, swallowing every last drop, absorbing.

When I'd finally sucked him dry, I turned away and howled at the sky like the Wolf Man had. For a long time that's all I could do, howl and scream and cry like the wild animal of the night which I'd become.

CHAPTER THIRTY-THREE

MR TALL and a handful of others from the Cirque Du Freak — including four Little People — arrived a bit later. I was sitting by Sam's side, too tired to howl any more, staring blankly into space, feeling his blood settle in my stomach.

"What's the story?" Mr Tall asked Mr Crepsley. "How did the Wolf Man get free?"

"I do not know, Hibernius," Mr Crepsley replied. "I have not asked and do not intend to, not for a night or two at least. Darren is in no fit shape for an interrogation."

"Is the Wolf Man dead?" Mr Tall asked.

"No," Mr Crepsley said. "I merely knocked him out."

"Thank heaven for small mercies," Mr Tall sighed. He clicked his fingers and the Little People chained up the unconscious Wolf Man. A van from the show pulled up and they bundled him into the back.

I thought about demanding the Wolf Man's death but what good would it have been? He wasn't evil, just naturally mad. Killing him would have been pointless and cruel.

When they'd finished with the Wolf Man, the Little People's attention turned to Sam's shredded remains.

"Hold on," I said, as they bent to pick him up and cart him away. "What are they going to do with Sam?"

Mr Tall coughed uncomfortably. "I, ah, rather imagine they intend to *dispose* of him," he said.

It took me a moment to realize what that meant. "They're going to *eat* him?" I shrieked.

"We can't just leave him here," Mr Tall reasoned, "and we don't have time to bury him. This is the easiest—"

"No," I said firmly.

"Darren," Mr Crepsley said, "we should not interfere with—"

"No!" I shouted, striding over to shove the Little People backwards. "If they want to eat Sam, they'll have to eat me first!"

The Little People stared at me wordlessly, with hungry green eyes.

"I think they'd be quite happy to accommodate you," Mr Tall said drily.

"I mean it," I growled. "I won't let them eat Sam. He deserves a proper burial."

"So that worms can devour him?" Mr Tall asked, then sighed when I glared at him, and shook his head irritably.

"Let the boy have his way, Hibernius," Mr Crepsley said softly. "You may return to the Cirque with the others. I will stay and help dig the grave."

"Very well," Mr Tall shrugged. He whistled and cocked a finger at the Little People. They hesitated, then backed away and grouped around the owner of the Cirque Du Freak, leaving me alone with the dead Sam Grest.

Mr Tall and his assistants left. Mr Crepsley sat down beside me.

"How are you?" he asked.

I shook my head. There was no simple answer to that.

"Do you feel stronger?"

"Yes," I said softly. Even though it hadn't been long since I'd drank Sam's blood, already I noticed a difference. My eyesight had improved, as had my hearing, and my battered body didn't hurt nearly as much as it should.

"You will not have to drink again for a long time," he said.

"I don't care. I didn't do it for me. I did it for Sam."

"Are you angry with me?" he asked.

"No," I sighed.

"Darren," he said, "I hope—"

"I don't want to talk about it!" I snapped. "I'm cold, sore, miserable and lonely. I want to think about Sam, not waste words on you."

"As you wish," he said, and began digging in the soil with his fingers. I dug beside him in silence for a few minutes, then paused and looked over.

"I'm a real vampire's assistant now, aren't I?" I asked.

He nodded sadly. "Yes. You are."

"Does that make you glad?"

"No," he said. "It makes me feel ashamed."

As I stared at him, confused, a figure appeared above us. It was the Little Person with the limp. "If you think you're taking Sam ..." I warned him, raising a dirt-encrusted hand. Before I got any further, he jumped into the shallow hole, stuck his wide, grey-skinned fingers into the soil, and clawed up large clumps.

"He's helping us?" I asked, puzzled.

"It seems like it," Mr Crepsley said, and laid a hand on my back. "Rest," he advised. "We can dig faster by ourselves. I will call you when it is time to bury your friend."

I saw sense in that, nodded, crawled out and lay down on the bank beside the quickly forming grave. After a while I shuffled out of the way and sat, waiting, in the shadows of the old railway station. Just me and my thoughts. And Sam's dark red blood on my lips and between my teeth.

CHAPTER THIRTY-FOUR

WE BURIED Sam without much ado – I couldn't think of anything fitting to say – and filled in the grave. We didn't camouflage it, so he'd be discovered by the police and given a real burial soon. I wanted his parents to be able to give him a proper send-off, but this would keep him safe from scavenging animals (and Little People) in the meantime.

We broke camp before dawn. Mr Tall told everybody there was a long trek ahead. Sam's disappearance would create a fuss, so we had to get as far away from here as possible.

I wondered, as we set off, what had become of R.V. Had he bled to death in the forest? Had he made it to a doctor in time? Or was he still running and screaming: "My hands! My hands!"?

I didn't care. Although he'd been trying to do the right thing, this was R.V.'s fault. If he hadn't gone messing with the locks on the Wolf Man's cage, Sam would be alive. I didn't hope R.V. was dead, but I didn't say a prayer for him either. I'd leave him to fate and whatever it had in store.

Evra sat beside me at the rear of a van as the Cirque pulled out. He started to say something. Stopped. Cleared his throat. Then he placed a bag on my lap. "I found that," he muttered.

"Thought you might want it."

Through stinging eyes I read the name – "Sam Grest" – then burst into tears and wept bitterly over it. Evra put his arms around me and held me tight and cried along with me.

"Mr Crepsley told me what happened," Evra mumbled eventually, recovering slightly and wiping his face clean. "He said you drank Sam's blood to keep his spirit alive."

"Apparently," I replied weakly, unconvinced.

"Look," Evra said, "I know how much you didn't want to drink human blood, but you did this for Sam. It was an act of goodness, not evil. You shouldn't feel bad for drinking from him."

"I guess," I said, then moaned at the memory and wept some more.

The day grew old, the Cirque Du Freak rolled on, but thoughts of Sam couldn't be left behind. As night closed upon us, we pulled over to the side of the road for a short break. Evra went to look for food and refreshments.

"Can I get you anything?" he asked.

"No," I said, my face pressed against the window pane. "I'm not hungry."

He started to leave.

"Wait a sec," I called him back.

There was a strange taste in my mouth. Sam's blood was still hot on my lips, salty and terrible, but that wasn't what had set the buds at the back of my tongue tingling. There was something I wanted which I'd never wanted before. For a handful of confusing moments I didn't know what it was. Then I placed the strange craving and managed the thinnest of smiles. I searched Sam's bag, but the jar must have been left behind when we broke camp.

Looking up at Evra, I wiped tears from my eyes, licked my lips, and asked in a voice which sounded a lot like that of a curious, smartass kid I once knew, "Do we have any pickled onions?"

TO BE CONTINUED…

To save a life, Darren Shan must risk his own,
by facing a creature of evil in the

TUNNELS OF BLOOD

Dare to read on ...

PROLOGUE

THE SMELL of blood is sickening. Hundreds of carcasses hang from silver hooks, stiff, shiny with frosty blood. I know they're just animals — cows, pigs, sheep — but I keep thinking they're human.

I take a careful step forward. Powerful overhead lights mean it's bright as day. I have to tread carefully. Hide behind the dead animals. Move slowly. The floor's slippery with water and blood, which makes progress even trickier.

Ahead, I spot him ... the vampire ... Mr Crepsley. He's moving as quietly as I am, eyes focussed on the fat man a little way ahead.

The fat man. He's why I'm here in this ice-cold abattoir. He's the human Mr Crepsley intends to kill. He's the man I have to save.

The fat man pauses and checks one of the hanging slabs of meat. His cheeks are chubby and red. He's wearing clear plastic gloves. He pats the dead animal — the squeaky noise of the hook as the carcass swings sets my teeth on edge — then begins whistling. He starts to walk again. Mr Crepsley follows. So do I.

Evra is somewhere far behind. I left him outside. No point the two of us risking our lives.

I pick up speed, moving slowly closer. Neither knows I'm

here. If everything works out as planned, they won't know, not until Mr Crepsley makes his move. Not until I'm forced to act.

The fat man stops again. Bends to examine something. I take a quick step back, afraid he'll spot me but then I see Mr Crepsley closing in. Damn! No time to hide. If this is the moment he's chosen to attack, I have to get nearer.

I sprint forward several metres, risking being heard. Luckily Mr Crepsley is entirely focussed on the fat man.

I'm only three or four metres behind the vampire now. I bring up the long butcher's knife which I've been holding down by my side. My eyes are glued to Mr Crepsley. I won't act until he does – I'll give him every chance to prove my terrible suspicions wrong – but the second I see him tensing to spring...

I take a firmer grip on the knife. I've been practising my swipe all day. I know the exact point I want to hit. One quick cut across Mr Crepsley's throat and that'll be that. No more vampire. One more carcass to add to the pile.

Long seconds slip by. I don't dare look to see what the fat man is studying. Is he never going to rise?

Then it happens. The fat man struggles to his feet. Mr Crepsley hisses. He gets ready to lunge. I position the knife and steady my nerves. The fat man's on his feet now. He hears something. Looks up at the ceiling – wrong way, fool! – as Mr Crepsley leaps. As the vampire jumps, so do I, screeching loudly, slashing at him with the knife, determined to kill ...

DARREN SHAN

CIRQUE DU FREAK

THE SAGA OF DARREN SHAN
BOOK 1

Darren Shan is just an ordinary schoolboy – until he gets an invitation to visit the Cirque Du Freak... until he meets Madam Octa... until he comes face to face with a creature of the night.

Soon, Darren and his friend Steve are caught in a deadly trap. Darren must make a bargain with the one person who can save Steve. But that person is not human and only deals in blood...

ISBN 0 00 675416-3

www.darrenshan.com